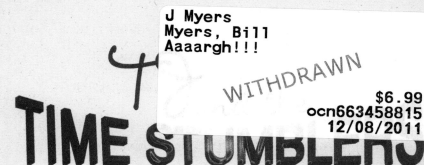

TIME STUMBLERS

BOOK 2
AAAARGH!!!

D1531270

Bill

Tyndale House Publishers, Inc.
Carol Stream, Illinois

Visit Tyndale's exciting Web site for kids at www.tyndale.com/kids.

Visit Bill Myers's Web site at www.billmyers.com.

TYNDALE and Tyndale's quill logo are registered trademarks of Tyndale House Publishers, Inc.

AAAARGH!!!

Designed by Stephen Vosloo

Edited by Sarah Mason

Published in association with the literary agency of Alive Communications, Inc., 7680 Goddard Street, Suite 200, Colorado Springs, CO 80920, www.alivecommunications.com.

For manufacturing information regarding this product, please call 1-800-323-9400.

Library of Congress Cataloging-in-Publication Data

Myers, Bill, date.
   AAAARGH!!! / Bill Myers.
      p. cm. — (TJ and the time stumblers ; bk. 2)
   ISBN 978-1-4143-3454-7 (sc)
      [1. Conduct of life—Fiction.   2. Cheating—Fiction.   3. Time travel—Fiction.
4. Junior high schools—Fiction.   5. Schools—Fiction.   6. Malibu (Calif.)—Fiction.]
I. Title.
   PZ7.M98234Aaf 2011
   [Fic]—dc22   2010029275

Printed in the United States of America

17   16   15   14   13   12   11
7   6   5   4   3   2   1

For the Kristi Toler-Harding family

CHAPTER ONE

Beginnings . . .

TIME TRAVEL LOG:
Malibu, California, October 19

Begin Transmission:
Time-travel pod still zworked. Subject is growing used to our presence. She barely groans when she sees us. Big-time improvement. Currently assisting her in studies, though she doesn't exactly appear grateful.

End Transmission

"WHAT ARE YOU DOING?!" TJ Finkelstein yelled

as she dropped the book she was reading and jumped up from her desk. "HERBY!"

Now, TJ really wasn't a yeller. But when your room is suddenly filled with two dozen pirates from the 1700s (and none of them are as cute as Johnny Depp), well, that's enough to make anybody a little irritable.

Actually, it wasn't the pirates that bothered TJ as much as their

cling-clang
clunk!

sword fighting.

"TUNA!?" she shouted.

And even that wasn't as bad as their

cling-clang
jab!
cling-clang

jab!

2

"AIIuIIuuH!"

falling down all wounded on her floor.

"Great!" she cried. "How am I going to get those bloodstains out of my carpet? HERBY!"

There was still no answer, except for the

"Hardee-har-har . . ."

of another pirate as he swung toward her on a rope.

She screamed and dropped to the floor as he flew past, missing her by inches. Scrambling back to her feet, she searched the room—ducking this sword, dodging that saber as the pirates continued to

Cling-clang

clunK!

Once again she shouted, "TUNA! HERBY! WHERE ARE YOU?!"

Suddenly two frightened heads popped out from under her bed. The good news was the heads were still attached to their bodies. (With all the swinging

swords and sabers, that *was* good news.) The first
belonged to Herby. He had long blond bangs and
was not the brightest candle on the birthday cake.
(Sometimes he couldn't even find the party.) The
second belonged to Tuna, who had red hair and was
sort of chubby. They were both a couple years older
than TJ and perfectly normal . . . except for the part
about them coming from the 23rd century.

The 23rd century?!

That's right. And don't worry about the shouting—
that was TJ's first reaction too. It was also her second
reaction and her third . . . and her reaction every
time she woke up in the morning to see them standing in line to use her bathroom. (Apparently even
23rd-century time travelers need to use the facilities.)

It seems she was the subject of their history proj-
ect back at their school. Someday she would grow
up to be a brilliant leader doing brilliant things (hard
to believe, since she was still having a hard time
opening her locker).

Anyway, the two boys had traveled back to her
time to observe her.

The only problem was they got stuck. Their time-
travel pod broke down and ran out of fuel. And
until they could fix it, TJ Finkelstein had become
their reluctant hostess. It wasn't bad enough that

she'd just moved to California from a small town in Missouri. Or that the kids at Malibu Junior High were the richest (and snobbiest) in the world. She also had to deal with all the catastrophes created by her brain-deprived friends from the 23rd century.

"What are you doing?" she demanded.

Tuna (aka Thomas Uriah Norman Alphonso the Third) cleared his throat. "You appeared to be having some difficulty with your *Treasure Island* book report."

"It's due tomorrow, and I haven't had a chance to—"

"Step lively, mateys! Comin' through!"

The boys ducked back under the bed and TJ jumped aside as two pirates rolled a heavy black cannon up to her window. She could only stare in disbelief.

Herby was the first to pop back out. Flipping his bangs to the side, he explained, "We figured the coolest way to read a book is to, like, live it."

TJ glanced around. "You mean to *watch* it, like a movie."

Suddenly a gnarled hand reached around and covered her mouth, while another shoved an old-fashioned pistol into her side. Her eyes widened in terror as she turned to see a pirate with a wooden leg and a parrot perched on his shoulder.

"Uh, no," Tuna corrected, "we mean to actually live it."

The pirate growled, "And who might ye be, missy? Someone out to steal me treasure?"

"Pieces of eight!" the parrot squawked.
"Pieces of eight!"

Of course TJ screamed: "Mmumoumrrmform-mumrormf!" (Which might have sounded more like *"Excuse me, I'd appreciate not dying at this particular time in my life!"* if his hand weren't still over her mouth.)

"Are you saying you wish for us to stop?" Tuna asked.

TJ glared at him.

"I think we should take that as a yes," Herby said.

TJ gave a huge nod.

"Well, all right, if you're certain." Tuna pulled out a giant Swiss Army Knife (the type sold at time-travel stores everywhere). He opened the blade labeled Story Amplifier and

Zibwa-zibwa-zibwa

absolutely nothing happened. (Well, except for the cool sound.)

"Try it again, dude!" Herby shouted.

Tuna shut the blade and reopened it. Again, nothing happened, except for the still very cool

Zibwa-zibwa-zibwa

Meanwhile, one of the pirates with the cannon at the window shouted, "Stand by!"

His partner produced a giant wooden match and yelled, "Standing by!"

Only then did TJ notice that the cannon wasn't just pointing out her window. It was pointing out her window directly at her neighbor Chad Steel's bedroom!

"Nuummmermumblemuffin!" she shouted. Only this time she made her point clearer by raising her foot high in the air and stomping hard onto the pirate's one good foot.

"ARGH!" he shouted, letting her go and jumping up and down on his other foot (which, unfortunately, was not there). So, having only a peg for a foot, he did a lot more

ker-plop-ing

onto the ground than jumping. And with all the
ker-plop-ing came a lot more *"ARGH!"*-ings followed
by a ton of *"Bleep-bleep-bleep, bleep-bleep-bleep"*-ings
(which is all pirates are allowed to scream in a
PG-rated book).

Meanwhile, the other two pirates were preparing
to fire the cannon.

"Ready!" the first pirate shouted.

TJ raced to the window. "Don't shoot! Don't
shoot!" She turned to the boys still under the bed.
"Tuna! Herby! Do something!"

"As you have no doubt observed," Tuna explained,
"our equipment is once again experiencing technical
difficulties."

"Ready!" the second pirate echoed his partner's
command as he struck the giant match. But before
he could light the cannon's fuse, TJ spun around and
blew it out.

He frowned. "What ye be doin' that for, missy?"

She twirled back to Tuna and Herby. "Hit it
on the ground again! Hit the knife thingy on the
ground!"

Once again the pirate lit a match and once again
she spun around and blew it out.

"ARGH," the pirate *argh*-ed. (He would have

thrown in a few *bleep*s of his own but figured his mother might be reading this book.)

Tuna called back to TJ, "I fail to see how hitting the knife upon the—"

"It's worked before!" Herby shouted at Tuna. "Give it a try."

The second pirate struck a third match, and this time blocking TJ from it, he managed to light the fuse. It started smoking and sputtering.

Tuna continued arguing with Herby. "I fail to see the logic in *thwack*-ing the Story Amplifier on the ground."

"Guys!" TJ shouted.

"That's how we fixed it before, dude."

"Guys!" TJ whirled back to the fuse, watching it burn toward the cannon.

"This is extremely expensive equipment," Tuna argued. "Such handling would be foolish and—"

"Aim!" the first pirate shouted.

"Aim!" the second pirate repeated as he adjusted the cannon so it would clearly destroy Chad's house.

"Fire!"

"Fire!"

Both men plugged their ears and closed their eyes . . . which gave TJ just enough time to throw herself at the cannon and *grrr, arrrr,* **ugghhh . . .**

move it 6¼ inches before it finally

k-blewie-ed

The good news was the cannonball missed Chad's house by mere inches. (Close, but when it comes to total demolition of a neighbor's house, every inch counts.)

The better news was Tuna finally agreed to

thwack, **thwack,** thwack

the knife on the floor until the Story Amplifier

Zibwa-zibwa-zibwa

DING!

finally shut down.

Suddenly everything in the room was back to normal. No fighting pirates, no shooting cannons. Everything was gone . . . well, except for one or two parrot feathers floating to the ground and the gentle sound of

whhhhhuuuuuuUUUUU . . .

a light evening breeze blowing through the new hole in TJ's bedroom wall. The new hole that was roughly the size of a very large cannonball.

* * * * *

It had been a rough day for Hesper Breakahart, too. Besides the usual problems that came with being a super-rich, super-spoiled, and super-famous TV star on the Dizzy Channel, she had a terrible headache. There were three whiny reasons for her suffering:

WHINY REASON #1
The thirteen-year-old beauty queen had found a split end in her perfectly styled and perfectly blonde (because it was perfectly dyed) hair.

But that catastrophe was nothing compared to

WHINY REASON #2
Hesper had nearly broken a nail—which is a danger you risk when your PTB (Personal Tooth

Brusher) calls in sick and you have to brush your teeth by yourself.

But even that was small potatoes (or in Hesper's case, very small portions of caviar) when compared to

WHINY REASON #3

She was still having to talk to the common people. (Insert gasp here.) That's right, the great Hesper Breakahart, star of stage, screen, and her own ego, actually had to pretend to like her fellow students.

It had all started last week when the new girl from Memphis—or Miami or whatever that Midwest state that starts with an *M* is called—embarrassed her in front of the entire school. For five terrifying minutes, every student at Malibu Junior High had heard Hesper's real thoughts broadcast through the school's PA system. Now they *all* knew how much she loathed them. (It's not that Hesper was a snob, but when you're as big a winner as she is, it's hard to ignore how big a loser everyone else is.)

So for the last week, she'd had to go around school telling those awful, average people how much she respected them (insert second gasp here). Talk about embarrassing. Talk about humiliating. It was almost as bad as when she had to share the cover of *Teen Idol* with some stupid brother band that everyone was all gaga over.

But now it was

PAYBACK TIME

Hesper Breakahart was going to think up a plan so nasty and so evil that TB—or BLT or whatever that new girl's name was—would wish she'd never been born.

"So what will it be?" Hesper's very best friend since forever asked while sitting at Hesper's feet. (All of Hesper's subjects—er, friends—sat at her feet. Usually around the pool, working on their tans.)

"I don't know," Hesper said, drawing her perfectly plucked eyebrows into a perfectly plucked frown.

"Make her drink regular tap water?" Hesper's other very best friend since forever asked. (When you're a TV star, you've got plenty of very best friends.)

"Take away her credit cards?" another very best friend asked.

"Make it so she can't get a pedicure for a whole month?"

All the girls shuddered.

"EEEEeeeewWW . . ."

"Oh, I know; I know," the first very best friend said.

Hesper turned to her. "Yes, er, um . . ."

"Elizabeth."

Hesper flashed her recently whitened, glow-in-the-dark-teeth smile. "Yes, of course it is. What's on your mind, um, er . . ."

"Elizabeth."

"Right."

Elizabeth didn't need Hesper to know her name. Just letting her hang at the pool and breathe the same air was enough. "You know how weird stuff seems to be happening whenever the new kid is around?"

"Yes," another very best friend since forever said, "like the book that flew across Mr. Beaker's class when she came into the room?"

Another very best friend (I told you she had plenty) added, "Or that dodgeball that made a U-turn and hit you when she was in PE?"

"Or how 'bout when she—?"

"Please, please." Hesper held up her perfectly manicured hand. "Must we always be talking about her?"

Elizabeth frowned. "But I thought—"

"We were talking about what *I* was going to do to her."

"Oh, right." Elizabeth glanced down, embarrassed. If there was one thing you didn't talk about when you were around Hesper Breakahart, it was other people.

Hesper reached out an understanding hand and patted Elizabeth on the head. "That's okay, um, er, whoever you are."

Another very best friend since forever spoke up. "What if *you* hired a private detective?"

Hesper turned to her, waiting for more.

"*You* could have him find some dirt on her for *you,* and then *you* could tell everybody what *you* learned."

"*I* could?" Hesper asked. She was already liking the plan. (Well, not so much the plan as the *star* of the plan.) "But where would *I* find a detective to do that for *me*?"

Elizabeth's hand shot up in the air. "I could do it! I could do it!"

Hesper scowled.

Immediately, Elizabeth realized her error. "That is, for *you*. I could do it for *you* so *you* could tell everybody what *you* learned."

"Hmm . . ." A smile slowly crept around the corners of Hesper's all-too-perfect lips. "I like that . . . what's-your-name. Yes, I like that a lot."

CHAPTER TWO

Temptations

TIME TRAVEL LOG:

Malibu, California, October 20

Begin Transmission:
Subject's gratitude has not improved. After receiving outloopish gift, she appears more gur-roid than ever. Cause unknown. Maybe she's allergic to parrots.

End Transmission

The sun was just rising as Chad Steel sat on his surfboard, waiting for the next set of waves to roll in. School wouldn't start for another hour. But that was okay. He never minded getting up early to surf. There were three things he loved about it:

1. The beauty and silence of being alone on the water.
2. Leaving his phone on the beach so he couldn't receive Hesper's calls.
3. The thrill of catching the right wave and working its power.
4. Leaving his phone on the beach so he couldn't receive Hesper's text messages.

Actually, that was four things, but Chad was a surfer, not a math geek. He'd leave the math (and the geekiness) to such brainiacs as

"How's my ten-four, Chad? Do you (sniff-sniff) *copy? Repeat, do you* (snort-snort) *copy?"*

Doug Claudlooper, who was currently speaking through Chad's earpiece. And if you couldn't tell it was Doug by all the *sniff-sniff*-ing and *snort-snort*-ing (Doug had a permanent case of hay fever), you could tell by the way he was waving at Chad from the beach like a madman (or in Doug's case, a mad scientist).

The reason was simple: he'd learned Chad was going to compete in the big surfing event this weekend and had convinced him to try out his newest invention:

The Lifter-Upper-a-Few-Inches-from-the-Water Surfboard

(All right, so he'd work on the name later.)

The point is, Doug had created a surfboard that had little jet engines built into the bottom. So whenever he pressed a button, the board would fire up and rise a few inches off the water. Without the extra friction, Chad would be able to do a lot more stunts and maneuvers during the championship.

But Chad had been skeptical. . . .

"I don't know," he said. "I don't think it's legal."

"It's only illegal if you *(sniff-sniff)* get caught," Doug said.

Chad still didn't like the idea, but since he was a nice guy (some said the nicest guy in school) and since Doug was a nobody nerd (some said the nerdiest nobody in school), he'd offered to help Doug and give the board a test run.

So here they were at sunrise, getting ready to try it out.

Chad looked ahead and saw the water starting to swell. He spoke into the headpiece. "Looks like we got a good set coming in."

"Roger that."

"It's coming in fast."

"Ready when you are."

Chad turned his board and started paddling toward shore. He felt the water lift the board. This was good. He paddled harder, making sure he would be on the breaking side. He glanced over his shoulder. The wave was just about to curl. Quickly, he scrambled to his feet.

"Okay," he shouted, "I'm up!"

"Commencing countdown (sniff). On my mark (snort). Five . . . Four . . . Three . . ."

The tube of water was building nicely. Chad cut the board to the right, picking up speed, making sure he stayed inside the pipe.

"Two . . . One . . ."

He snapped the board to the left. Now he was in the perfect position, racing down the wall. "Let's do it!" he shouted.

"Beginning ignition sequence."

"Hurry!"

There was no answer.

"Doug, anytime you feel like—"

WHOosh!

Chad felt the board vibrate under his feet as the jets fired and pushed it up, one inch . . . two inches.

Perfect. Now there was no friction on the water and Chad could begin all kinds of maneuvers. There was only one problem. The

whooOOSH

grew louder.

The board rose three inches . . . four inches . . .

"Okay," Chad shouted, "that's enough!"

WHOOoOOOSH

Ten inches . . . twenty inches . . . then twenty *feet*!

Chad yelled, "Shut it down! Doug, shut it down!"

"I'm . . . (crackle-crackle) . . . *unsure* . . . (crinkle-crinkle) . . ."

Chad pressed the receiver to his ear. "You're breaking up! Doug, can you hear me?"

Chad heard only one word. That is if you count

"Uh-oh!"

as a word.

Suddenly he shot straight up into the sky

!"

!

!

H

H

H

H

G

U

"A

in a space shuttle kinda way.

Now, to call the experiment a failure really wasn't fair. . . .

Granted, the police did receive a lot of UFO

sightings—actually, UFS (Unidentified Flying Surfboard) sightings:

"Officer, it was like this giant surfboard was shooting across the horizon!"

"Step out of the car, sir. We need to check your breath for alcohol."

And the United States Air Force did have to scramble a couple of fighter jets to shoot down an enemy missile:

"General, you won't believe it. There's nothing up here but . . . but . . ."

"But what, pilot?"

"A kid on a surfboard!"

"Return to base immediately for mental evaluation!"

(All right, I might have exaggerated a little, but when you're flying 100 miles into the air . . . well, okay, 30 miles . . . well, all right, 30 feet—things can feel a lot more dramatic.)

The good news was the board finally stopped flying.

The bad news was what goes up must come

down.

SplAsh!

But at least Chad was alive. He wasn't crazy about landing in the ocean halfway to Hawaii. (Okay, that's another exaggeration; so sue me.)

But he was alive.

* * * * *

"All right, guys!" TJ stood in the hallway, wearing her backpack and calling up to the attic door. "Guys, who wrote this? *Guys*?"

The *this* was a typed, 20-page book report she held in her hands.

The *guys* were, of course, Tuna and Herby.

"I'm not leaving for school 'til someone answers me!"

Finally the attic door creaked open an inch and a pair of eyes appeared.

"Come down here," TJ demanded.

The door opened another inch and another pair of eyes appeared.

"Now!"

Reluctantly, the boys opened the door the rest of the way and floated down, cross-legged, to greet her. It always weirded her out to see them floating like that. But that weirdness was nothing compared to the weirder weirdness she was about to be weirded out by.

TRANSLATION: *Things might get a little weird.*

She waved the book report at them. "I found this on my desk this morning."

"You don't say," Tuna said, pretending to be surprised.

TJ simply looked at him. He was as bad an actor as he was a time traveler.

"Any idea where it came from?" she asked.

Herby floated to her other side and looked.
"Cool. Maybe it was, like, the book report fairy."

She blew the hair out of her eyes in frustration.
"Which one of you wrote this?"

"Perhaps you typed it yourself," Tuna said.

"In my sleep?"

"You've never heard of sleep typing?" Herby
asked. "It can be a terrible thing."

"Guys?!"

"Your Dude-ness," Herby said, "didn't you say you
had a gargantuan book report due today?"

"Right, but—"

"And with all the distractions Tuna caused last
night, we figured—"

"Excuse me," Tuna interrupted. "I was not the one
responsible for last evening's distractions."

"You were too."

"Was not."

"Were too."

"Was—"

"Guys!"

"—not."

"Were—"

"GUYS!"

They came to a stop.

Once again she raised the paper. "I can't hand this in."

"Why not?" Herby asked. "Is it too short?"

"I can't hand it in because I didn't write it."

"So?"

"So that's cheating."

The boys looked at each other, puzzled.

"Even if it's well typed?" Herby asked.

"Even if it's well typed," TJ sighed.

"Even if Robert Louis Stevenson wrote it for you?" Tuna asked.

"Even if Robert Louis . . . Wait a minute. Robert Louis Stevenson, the author, wrote this?"

The boys grinned in pride.

Tuna explained, "We time-ported him up to our attic last night."

TJ could barely speak. "Robert Louis Stevenson, the author of *Treasure Island*, wrote a book report on his own book . . . *for me*?"

"Correct," Tuna said. "We bribed him with food items unavailable in his era—a Big Mac and a strawberry shake."

"And a Happy Meal toy, dude. Don't forget the Happy Meal toy."

Before TJ could respond, her backpack started to move.

"Excuse me, Your Dude-ness, but is your backpack alive?"

"Don't be torked," Tuna scoffed. "Living back-packs were not invented until the year 2104."

Next, the backpack started to wiggle.

(Remember that weirdness that's supposed to be happening? Well, buckle up.)

Actually, the wiggling backpack wasn't as weird as the way it started screaming,

"Shiver me timbers! Shiver me timbers!"

Not to be outdone, TJ let out her own scream. She slipped off the pack as fast as she could and dropped it to the floor, where it kept right on wiggling.

To make matters worse, her cute little sister, Dorie, called from downstairs in her cute little sister voice. "TJ, you okay?"

"Pieces of eight!" the backpack cried. **"Pieces of eight! Squawk!"**

"TJ?"

TJ would have loved to answer, but it's hard answering when you're busy having a nervous breakdown.

"Open it," Tuna whispered to Herby. "Open the backpack!"

"You open it," Herby whispered back.

"TJ?" Cute little sister Dorie started up the stairs. "Is everything okay?"

TJ stared at the moving backpack, then looked to the stairs, her panic growing. This was the last thing her sister needed to see.

"TJ?"

"Do something!" she hissed. "Guys?!"

Without a word, Tuna reached into his pocket for his Swiss Army Knife. Before TJ could stop him (things never seemed to go right with that contraption), he opened the Time Freezer Blade and

ZZOO . . . o . . . o . . . . a . . . . . a . . . . . a . . . . h . . . . h . . . .

Dorie and everything around her turned to slow motion.

"T . . . . J . . . ."

Dorie was still climbing the stairs, but by the time she arrived, TJ would either:

    A) Be an old lady

B) Be eaten alive by the alien backpack

C) Find the courage to reach down and open the backpack herself.

It was a tough call, but TJ chose C.

She reached down, quickly unzipped the pack, and was suddenly hit with a faceful of feathers. Last night's parrot flew out squawking and shrieking. (Though it was hard to hear over TJ's own squawking and shrieking. Something about a parrot appearing in your backpack at 7:40 in the morning will do that to a person.)

The bird began flying around their heads, crying, **"Shiver me timbers! Shiver me timbers!"**

Meanwhile, Dorie continued up the stairs. "Whaaa aat'ssssss . . . . goooooooooo . . . ."

"Guys, do something!" TJ shouted.

" . . . . iiiiiiiing . . . ."

The good news was Tuna had already pulled open another blade on his Swiss Army Knife. Once again it started making all those cool

zibwa-zibwa-zibwa

noises.

The bad news was

"Pieces of eight! Pieces of eight!"

nothing happened. (Well, except that Dorie finally appeared at the top of the stairs.)

". . . . . onnnn . . . ."

"Give it a *thwack*!" Herby shouted. "Give it a *thwack*!"

"I'm *thwack*-ing; I'm *thwack*-ing!" Tuna shouted as he

thwack, *thwack*, *thwack-ed*

it against the side of the wall.

"*Guys!*"

". . . . . uuuuuuuup . . . ."

Finally, after one last *thwack*, the parrot

Zibwa-zibwa-zibwa

DING!

disappeared.

That was the good news. But as TJ had already

learned, with these guys there would always be some
bad. This time it came in the form of a

RAWHHH-SCREEEETCH!

RAWHHH-SCREEEETCH!

flying pterodactyl.

"A pterodactyl?" she shouted. "You turned the
parrot into a pterodactyl?"

"Please," Tuna said, "there's no reason to shout."

"THERE'S A FLYING DINOSAUR IN MY
HALLWAY!"

"Well, all right, perhaps there is a small reason."

". . . . . .heeeeeeeeeeerrre . . . . ?"

Slowly, Dorie began turning her head. Any
minute she would see what was going on. Although
Tuna and Herby would be invisible to her, the pterodactyl would not. And although Dorie was pretty
easygoing, something about a flying dinosaur in the
house could send her into a screaming fit . . . which
could cause older sister Violet to appear and do the
same. . . . which could bring Dad upstairs to have a
major heart attack (since dads are even less fond of
flying dinosaurs than screaming sisters).

"Shiver me timbers! Shiver me timbers! SQUAWK!"

Once again Tuna *thwack*ed the blade and once again it:

zibwa-zibwa-zibwa

DING-ed!

This time the pterodactyl disappeared. So did the parrot. Finally everything was back to normal . . . well, except for a handful of colorful feathers floating down to the floor. Oh, and cute little Dorie still moving at about *1/390,234* miles per hour.

TJ spun back to Tuna and Herby. "What was that about?" she demanded. "And how come the bird came back?"

Tuna answered, "Apparently the time-space continuum was juxtaposed in such a nonlinear fashion that—"

TJ held up her hand. "English, please."

"Oh yes, certainly." He cleared his throat and carefully explained, "You've got me."

TJ gave him a look.

He gave her a shrug. Then, opening the Time Freezer Blade, he pointed it at her sister and

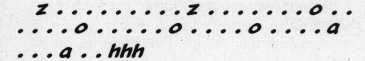

Z . . . . Z . . . . O . .
. . . . O . . . . . O . . . O . . . . a
. . . a . . hhh

everything returned to normal.

"You okay?" little Dorie squeaked in her little six-year-old voice.

"I'm fine, Squid," TJ said, scooping up her back-pack and heading past her. "Come on; we'll be late."

Dorie nodded and followed. "You gonna take me swimming right after school like you promised?"

"Sure."

"Great," she said, skipping down the stairs after her. "'Cause Dad won't let me go in the ocean by myself."

"Guess he figures one dead Finkelstein a year is enough."

It was supposed to be a joke. Their mother had died almost a year ago, which was one of the reasons their father had packed them up and moved to California. But even as she said it, TJ realized it wasn't funny. She was definitely on edge from her little encounter upstairs.

"TJ?" Dorie asked.

"Yeah?"

"Is that a feather in your hair?"

TJ reached up to her head and pulled off a bright green parrot feather.

Dorie looked at her. "Are you sure everything's okay?"

TJ shoved the feather into her pocket and opened the front door. "Everything's fine, Squid, perfectly normal. Let's go."

And the truth was TJ wasn't lying. Because for her, all this craziness *was* perfectly normal. Unfortunately, her latest perfectly normal would seem even more perfectly normal compared to the perfectly normal she was about to experience, which would be anything but normal.

TRANSLATION: *You guessed it: things will be getting a bit un-normal.*

CHAPTER THREE

Temptations x 2

TIME TRAVEL LOG:

Malibu, California, October 20–supplemental

Begin Transmission:
Stopped by subject's school to check up on her.
(Ahh . . .) Problems increasing. (Ahh . . . ahhh . . .)
Also afraid from what happened I may be allergic to
either salt or (ahh . . . ahhh . . . CHOO!) pepper.

End Transmission

"Thelma Jean?"

TJ was never fond of hearing her real name spoken. (With a name like hers, who could blame her?)

"Thelma Jean Finkelstein?"

She was even less fond of hearing her entire name. (Wouldn't you be?)

"Thelma Jean Finkelstein, may I see you a moment?"

And when it came from the lips of a teacher like Miss Grumpaton (who had a frown tattooed on her forehead so she could look mean even when she slept), TJ knew she was in trouble.

The rest of the class had left for lunch, so it was just the two of them in the room. TJ approached the desk. "Yes, Miss Grumpaton?"

"Why did I not receive your book report this morning?"

"Oh, I, um, er . . . I'm still working on it."

"Young lady, there are no late assignments in my class. You either hand the assignment in on time or you get a zero."

TJ could feel the weight of the 20-page book report still in her backpack. (At least she hoped it was the book report and not a parrot.)

"Hey, JT?"

She turned to see Elizabeth, one of Hesper's best friends since forever, standing at the door. "Are you coming to eat lunch with us or what?"

TJ glanced around the room to see who she was

talking to. But since there was no one there but her, she turned back and asked, "Me? You want *me* to eat at your table?"

"Well, of course, silly." Elizabeth flashed her every-tooth-in-place-thanks-to-a-$100,000-orthodontist-bill smile.

Needless to say, TJ was suspicious. (You'd have to have the IQ of a turtle not to be.) But before she could ask any more questions, Miss Grumpaton cleared her throat.

"Well?" the teacher asked.

TJ looked back at her and repeated, "I'm sorry; my report's just not ready."

"But you do have some of it, correct?"

"Well, yes, sure . . . sort of."

Now, to be honest, that really wasn't a lie. After all, she did have the pen she was going to write the report with, and she did have the paper she was going to write the report on, so technically she did have *part of the report* she was going to write with her.

"Since you're new," Miss Grumpaton said, "and since you made a complete ninny out of that Hesper Breakahart last week . . ." She lowered her voice and shook her head. "Honestly, I can't stand that girl. Probably because she reminds me so much of myself one or two years ago."

TJ nodded, thinking, *Now who's not telling the truth?*

Miss Grumpaton continued. "So, for this one time, I will allow you to hand in what you have completed and I will give you partial credit."

The report in TJ's backpack suddenly weighed even more.

"Well?" Miss Grumpaton said. "It's either that or get an F."

"Come on, BJ." Elizabeth motioned. "Give it to her and let's go."

TJ hesitated. She knew handing in the report was cheating . . . but she also knew she wanted to pass the class.

"JB, come on."

And sitting at Hesper and Elizabeth's table meant sitting with (insert dreamy sigh here) Chad Steel.

"I'm waiting, young lady," Miss Grumpaton said.

Finally, going against everything she knew was right (and now demonstrating the IQ of a turtle *in need of a brain transplant*), TJ slipped off her backpack, unzipped it, and pulled out the 20-page, single-spaced, typed book report.

"Wow!" Elizabeth said, stepping closer to look.

"You wrote this?" Miss Grumpaton asked.

TJ motioned toward her name at the top of the

paper and gave another not-quite-the-truth answer. "That's my name right there."

"My, oh, my," Miss Grumpaton said, flipping through the pages. "This is quite a report."

TJ swallowed nervously. Well, she tried to swallow nervously. But it's hard to swallow any type of way when your mouth is as dry as hot desert sand cooked in the toaster and blown dry by a hair dryer . . . set on high.

TRANSLATION: *It was dry.*

Miss Grumpaton looked at TJ and smiled (which got really confusing with her perma-frown tattoo). "Well done, my girl. Very well done. It appears I shall have some interesting reading this evening." Then, with a wave of her fossilized hand, she dismissed TJ.

The two girls left the room. Already TJ could feel the weight of guilt about what she'd done. It was so great she barely heard Elizabeth as they headed down the hall.

"That's incredible," Elizabeth was saying. "A 20-page book report."

"Yeah," TJ mumbled.

"You're just full of surprises, aren't you, TD?"

TJ looked up. "Hm?" Then shaking her head, she answered, "No, not really."

"Oh yeah, *really*. It's like every time you do something, it's weird and mysterious."

TJ laughed nervously—the type of laugh that's just a little too long and just a little too high . . . and just a little too suspicious.

Elizabeth lowered her voice. "You're not like some witch or something, are you? I mean some of this stuff could be right out of a Hairy Potty book."

"Me?" Another laugh, a little longer, a little higher, as they turned the corner and approached TJ's locker. "I'm just your average, run-of-the-mill girl from Missouri."

"Missouri? Is that like a state or something?"

TJ looked at her.

"I mean, it's not like a code name for some alien spaceship, is it?"

"Trust me," TJ said as they arrived at her locker and she dialed the combination, "there's absolutely nothing special about me." Without looking, she opened her locker door and slipped off her backpack.

"Oh, really?" Elizabeth said.

"Really. I'm just your average, all-American girl."

"Who just happens to have a boy stuffed in her locker?"

TJ turned to her locker and gasped. Elizabeth was right. There was a boy inside! But not just any boy. This kid looked like he was wearing clothes right out of the 18th century.

"Who . . . who are you?" TJ stuttered.

"I'm Jim Hawkins," he said, touching the brim of his hat. "Cabin boy on the good ship *Hispaniola*."

TJ blinked. Jim Hawkins was the cabin boy in *Treasure Island*! No way! It couldn't be!

"You wouldn't happen to know where I can find Long John Silver, would you?"

Without a word, TJ slammed the locker shut. She turned to Elizabeth and gave a nervous giggle.

Elizabeth shook her head. "Those clothes are sooo out of fashion."

TJ nodded.

"So who is he?" Elizabeth asked.

"Uh, um, Jim. My cousin. He's visiting."

The boy began

bang, bang, bang-ing

from inside the locker.

"Miss? . . . Excuse me, miss?"

"Your cousin?" Elizabeth asked skeptically.

"Right. Cousin Jimmy. He wanted to check out my school."

bang, bang, bang

"Excuse me . . . miss?"

"So . . . ," TJ said, trying to shout over the noise. "What say we grab some lunch? I'm starved."

bang, bang, bang

Without another word, she turned and quickly headed down the hall.

Fortunately, Elizabeth followed, staying glued to her side. Unfortunately, she still had a couple more questions to ask.

QUESTION #1:

"So if your cousin wants to see the school, how come he's locked in your locker?"

TJ shrugged. "He's just weird that way."

Elizabeth nodded and got around to

QUESTION #2:

"So . . . does that make him a witch, too—or just a sorcerer?"

* * * * *

The only good thing about sitting at the cool kids' table with Elizabeth and Hesper Breakahart was Chad Steel. It's not that she liked Chad or anything. I mean, other than him being the hottest guy in school and one of the sweetest boys she'd ever met, she never gave him a second thought.

A first thought, yes. Every five or six seconds, you bet. But nothing more.

They were simply neighbors who occasionally spoke to each other (whenever she could remember how to speak in front of him) or gave nods when they passed each other in the hall (whenever she could remember how to walk in front of him).

Besides, he was already spoken for by Hesper Breakahart. And after the way TJ embarrassed Hesper last week, it was important that TJ do everything she could to stay on the superstar's good side.

"So, um, er, new girl," Hesper said as one of her best friends opened an unflavored yogurt carton for her. (Hesper hated getting her hands dirty, and we all know the chances of getting a speck of yogurt on you when you peel back those dreadful foil lids.) "I hear you're really good at writing reports."

"She's better than good. She's really, *really* good," Elizabeth said as she opened her own unflavored yogurt . . . along with every other girl at the table. It wasn't much of a lunch, but imitation is the sincerest form of flattery, and Hesper definitely liked to be flattered.

TJ stole a look at Chad, pleased to see he was eating a triple-decker hamburger with everything on it.

Elizabeth continued. "She's so good, it's almost like she has magical powers." She gave TJ a knowing look, like they had some secret between them. TJ glanced away, pretending not to notice.

Hesper turned to TJ and smiled her dazzling smile. "Maybe you could give me some pointers on writing a report sometime?"

TJ gave a shrug. "Sure."

"Like tonight?"

TJ nearly choked on her peanut butter and jelly sandwich. "Tonight?"

"Yes, I've got a history report due, but I have this dreadful hangnail." Hesper held out her hand. "See?"

The other girls moved in, taking a closer look, *ooh*-ing and *aah*-ing in sympathy.

With a quiver in her voice, Hesper continued. "And until it heals, I just don't think I'll be able to write a single word."

"Ooh . . ."

"Aah . . ."

"In fact, you may have to write the entire report."

TJ fumbled for her milk carton to wash down her sandwich.

"Do you think you could do that?" Hesper asked, fighting back the tears.

All the girls at the table turned to TJ, fighting back their own tears.

TJ swallowed. To say no to Hesper would put her back on the diva's enemy list. But to write the paper for her would definitely be cheating.

And yet . . . cheating hadn't been so hard with Miss Grumpaton. In fact, the old lady seemed pretty impressed.

TJ watched as a single tear tracked down Hesper's perfectly made-up cheek. She looked back to the other girls and, you guessed it, saw the same tears on their same cheeks. And although it went against everything she knew was right, TJ finally nodded. "I might be able to help a little, sure."

"Yippee!" Hesper cried, throwing her arms around TJ.

"Yippee!" the other girls cried, throwing their arms around each other.

"My secretary will call you about the details," Hesper said, her tear suddenly disappearing as she returned to her yogurt.

Of course the other girls also returned to their yogurts, chittering and chattering about how lucky TJ was to be able to help Hesper. But the truth was TJ did not feel so lucky. She felt even less lucky when she glanced down at the salt and pepper shakers on the table. Because there, amid the little holes on the top of each shaker, was a set of tiny eyes. One set of tiny eyes that looked exactly like it belonged to Herby, and another set that looked exactly like it belonged to Tuna.

"Guys," she whispered, "what are you doing here?"

The salt and pepper shakers blinked.

"Are you spying on me?"

Elizabeth turned from Hesper and asked, "What's that, TB?"

"Oh, nothing." TJ smiled.

When she was sure it was safe, she turned back

to the salt and pepper shakers and demanded,
"Go home!"

More blinking.

"Go home *now*!"

Elizabeth turned back, her smile wilting slightly.
"I'm sorry?"

Again TJ smiled. "Oh . . . no, not you."

Elizabeth nodded, looking around the table before
returning to Hesper.

TJ glared back at the boys, but they still refused to
answer.

"All right, fine!" She reached for the saltshaker
with one hand and the pepper with the other. "If you
won't go home . . ." She turned them upside down
and began to shake.

"Your Dude-ness!" the saltshaker screamed.

TJ shook harder.

"I'm getting nauseated!" the pepper shaker cried.

"Me too," the saltshaker yelled. "I'm gonna hurl!"

By now everyone was looking around the table to
see who was yelling. Only Elizabeth, who stared at the
shakers, seemed to make some sort of connection.

"Say, BLT?" she asked. "Why are you salt and
peppering your peanut butter and jelly sandwich?"

Instantly, TJ stopped. But before she could answer

AAAARGH!!!

krinkle . . . krackle

POOF!

Tuna and Herby morphed themselves back into
normal people. Well, if you call 23rd-century time
travelers standing on the cafeteria table in their silver
time-travel suits "normal."

The good news was only TJ could see them.

The bad news was this didn't stop her from yelling, "Will you go home?!"

"What's that, um, er, new girl?" Hesper asked.

TJ looked to her, trying to smile but failing
miserably.

"Did you have something to contribute to our
conversation?"

TJ shook her head and looked down to her
sandwich.

"Good," Hesper said. "Just stick to writing papers
and leave intelligent conversation to us."

The girls giggled at what was supposed to be
humor. TJ felt her cheeks growing hot and nodded.
She stole a look at Chad, who seemed anything but
amused by the comment.

Unfortunately, Hesper wasn't exactly finished.

"I mean, since when do folks from Misery, or whatever state you're from, have anything important
to say?"

More tittering by the girls.

More blushing by TJ.

And more scowling by Chad.

But Herby had heard enough. Kneeling on the
table, he grabbed TJ's milk carton. Of course, he
was invisible, so all the kids saw was a milk carton
mysteriously float off the table and rise above
Hesper's head.

"Herby, don't!" TJ cried.

Everyone watched in amazement.

"Tuna, stop him!"

Tuna fumbled for his Swiss Army Knife. But he
was too late. Herby tilted the carton of milk and
poured. The liquid splashed out and was just inches
from Hesper's head when Tuna opened the Time
Freezer Blade and

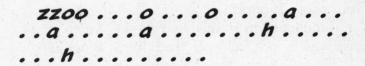

everything and everyone dropped into slow motion.

Everything and everyone but Tuna, Herby, and TJ.

TJ leaped to her feet and shouted at them. "What are you doing?! I told you to stay home. Why did you come to school?"

"We have an emergency, Your Dude-ness."

"I don't care about your emergency. There's no reason . . ." She pointed at the milk slowly falling from the carton. "You just can't . . . Why are you . . . ?"

"Didn't you hear what torked things she was saying about you?" Herby asked.

"Well, yes, but . . . I mean, it's Hesper Breakahart; what do you expect?"

Tuna stuck his finger into the slowly falling stream of milk and gave it a taste. "I expected it to be a lot creamier."

"That's because it's nonfat," Herby explained.

TJ blew the hair out of her eyes. "What kind of emergency?"

Tuna answered, "You must accompany us back to your house at once!"

TJ motioned to Hesper. By now the stream of milk was an inch from her head. "What about her?"

"We gotta hurry, Your Dude-ness!" Herby insisted.

And before TJ could protest, Tuna pulled out two knife blades. The Transporter Blade

chugga-**chugga**-*chugga*

BLING

which sent them back to her house, and the Time
Freezer Blade

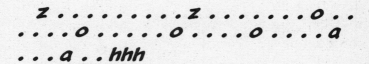

which returned everything to normal. Well, except
for the milk that suddenly drenched Hesper's head.

"MY HAIR!" she cried, "MY BEAUTIFULLY CUT
AND EXPENSIVELY STYLED HAIR!"

And while all the girls made a big fuss (and
poured milk over their own heads), Elizabeth noticed
something very strange. . . .

The new girl had disappeared. Vanished into
thin air.

CHAPTER FOUR

Crystal Ball . . . 23rd-Century Style

TIME TRAVEL LOG:

Malibu, California, October 20—supplemental

Begin Transmission:

Subject unreceptive to marriage proposal. No big quod-quod. She may come around . . . in two or three centuries! Sigh . . .

End Transmission

TJ stood inside her room with her hands on her hips. "So what was so important that you had to drag me away from my friends?" she demanded.

"Friends?" Tuna snorted. "You want them as friends?"

"Well, no, not really. But I don't want them as enemies, either."

"Your Dude-ness, that wannabe human was majorly zworking you!"

"Her name is Hesper Breakahart . . . and she just happens to be the most popular teenager in all of America!"

"Who will be completely forgotten in 10 years," Tuna said. "She's not even in the history holographs."

Herby nodded. "Whereas you, Your Dude-ness, are gonna be remembered forever for all the cool things you'll do."

"But what about now?" she argued.

"Now you are laying the foundation for what you'll become," Tuna explained. "Someone great who will end world hunger, eliminate diseases—"

"—and bring back the hula hoop!" Herby added brightly. Then, just as quickly, he deflated and said, "At least you were."

TJ turned to him. "What do you mean?"

Without a word, Tuna opened another blade of the Swiss Army Knife, and

buurringgg

ZAP!

the entire room was filled with babies. There were
hundreds of them crying and screaming.

"What's going on?" TJ shouted over the noise.

"It's a hologram," Tuna shouted back.

"Of what?"

"A Starving Room."

"A what?"

"In the future, it's where they'll put all the babies
who are starving to death."

TJ looked around the room in astonishment. It
was true. All the children there were starving. Some
were so skinny, they looked like skeletons with skin
stretched over their bones. It was hard to tell which
was worse—the way they looked or the way they
kept screaming and whimpering.

"But you said I was going to change all that!"
TJ shouted.

"You were," Tuna agreed, "until you . . ."

"Until I what?"

"Until you cheated with that book report."

"What?!" TJ motioned around the room. "How could a little cheating do all this?"

"You changed your future," Tuna said.

"How?"

He reopened the blade and

buurringg

ZAP!

the three of them were standing at the back of an auditorium full of clapping people. Onstage, an 18-year-old version of TJ, dressed in a plastic garbage bag, was receiving a certificate.

"What's this about?" TJ asked.

Tuna leaned toward her and explained, "Miss Grumpaton was so impressed by your report that she helped you acquire a writing scholarship to a top college."

TJ frowned. "But isn't that a good thing?"

"Yes and no. The good news is that garbage bags will be totally out of fashion in two years."

"And the bad news?" TJ asked.

"Pieces of eight! Pieces of eight!"

All three ducked as the parrot suddenly appeared

and flew just above their heads, then circled the audience.

"You still don't have that story thingy fixed?" TJ complained.

Herby shrugged. "We're waiting for parts."

Tuna pulled out the Story Amplifier Blade and tried to

Zibwa-zibwa-Zibwa

remove the bird. But nothing happened. He turned to TJ and shrugged. "Well, at least it's not that awful—"

RAWHHH-SCREEEETCH!

"PTERODACTYL!" all three cried in unison. After another

Zibwa-zibwa-Zibwa

and a few

thwack, thwack, thwacks

the pterodactyl finally

DING!

disappeared and everything was back to normal.
Well, except for the dinosaur drool on the heads of
several members of the audience.

"And the bad news?" TJ repeated. "You said there
was some bad news?"

"Right. Hang on." Tuna opened up the first blade
again and

buurringg

ZAP!

all three were transported to a college library. Not far
from them, a college-age version of TJ stood talking
to another student. After glancing nervously over her
shoulder, she slipped the student a wad of cash.

"What am I doing?" TJ whispered to the guys.

"You're buying a report from someone who wrote
it for you," Tuna said.

"I'm *what?*"

Herby explained, "Everyone went so gam-gam for

your writing that you had to keep cheating in college, too."

A sinking feeling filled TJ's stomach. "You mean I had to keep cheating to cover up my cheating?"

"Exactly."

"And it gets worse," Tuna said. He shut and reopened the blade.

buurringg

ZAP!

Suddenly all three were standing in a wedding chapel watching TJ get married. She was dressed in a beautiful white gown and veil.

"Wow," TJ whispered to the guys, "I look great."

Herby nodded. "Majorly smoot!"

But Tuna was looking at his knife, scowling. "That's not right. This isn't your—"

TJ didn't bother to listen. She quickly circled around to get a look at her future husband. The first thing she noticed was his height. He was about as tall as Herby. The second thing she noticed was his hair. It was as long and blond as Herby's. The third thing she noticed was

"AUGHHhhhhhh!"

(that, of course, would be TJ screaming)

it *was* Herby!

She spun around to the two boys and shouted, "What am I doing marrying Herby?!"

Tuna looked up from his knife and glared at his partner. "Herby?"

"HERBY?!" she shrieked.

"Sorry." He shrugged. "I was just falooping around and programmed it into the knife for fun."

TJ let out a huge sigh of relief. "So this really isn't my future?"

Tuna shook his head. "Absolutely not."

Herby added, "But if you wanted it to be—"

"Sorry, Herby," she interrupted. "No sale."

Once again, Herby seemed to deflate. "Sure, I get it. That's how you feel . . . at least for now."

"At least forever," she said.

Tuna reopened the blade and

buurringg

ZAP!

the three of them stood in a rich, expensive office watching a middle-aged TJ madly typing something from a book.

"What's this?" TJ asked as they approached her older image at the desk.

Tuna explained, "Your high grades in college brought you lots of money to write books. But because you were never any good, you had to steal from other authors."

"You mean I was cheating again?" TJ said.

Herby nodded. "You had to."

TJ scowled, then looked around at the fancy office. "But . . . I was successful, right?"

"That depends on how you define success." Tuna shut the knife, reopened it, and

buurringg

ZAP!

they were back to the room of starving and screaming babies.

Tuna continued his explanation. "Because you

became an author, someone other than you became president."

Slowly TJ put the pieces together. "So I wasn't there to stop world hunger."

"Precisely."

"And all of this will happen just because I cheated one time?" she asked.

Tuna answered, "Every action builds upon every other action."

Herby added, "Little wrongs create major quod-quods."

"But—" TJ turned to the boys, frowning—"it was your idea. You were the ones who told me to cheat."

Tuna looked to the ground. "And we were wrong."

"Majorly wrong," Herby agreed.

"More than majorly wrong; outloopishly wrong."

"Majorly, outloopishly—"

"Majorly, *majorly*, outloopishly—"

"All right, I get it." TJ raised her hand. "You were wrong."

The boys nodded. "Right!"

TJ sighed and looked around the room. "So there's nothing I can do to change this?"

Tuna and Herby traded glances.

As the babies continued to cry, TJ felt herself growing sick to her stomach. This really was her fault.

"There's nothing I can do to fix this?" she repeated hoarsely.

Finally Herby answered. "Yes, there is."

She looked at him, waiting for more.

Tuna explained, "You must tell Miss Grumpaton that you cheated."

If she felt sick before, she felt like calling an ambulance now. Tell Miss Grumpaton what she'd done? Forget the ambulance—call the local undertaker.

Suddenly her cell phone rang. She pulled it from her pocket and answered, "Hello?"

"TJ?" It was little Dorie. "Where are you?"

"I'm at home. Where are you?" TJ asked.

"At school. You were supposed to pick me up, remember?"

TJ frowned.

"We were going to the beach? You were taking me swimming."

"Oh, right. Sorry." She glanced at her watch, surprised at how much time had passed. "Hang on, Squid. I'll be right there." She closed her cell and turned to the guys. "I'd love to stick around, but I have to do something."

Herby motioned to the crying babies. "What about them?"

TJ looked around the room. "I feel terrible. And I think I know what you're saying, but . . ."

"But what?" Tuna asked.

"There's *no way* I can go to Miss Grumpaton."

Disappointment filled the boys' faces.

"Come on," she said. "You guys are smart. You'll figure out some other way to fix this."

They both stared at her.

"It was just one time," she argued. "Lots of kids cheat."

They continued to stare.

She blew her breath out and sighed. "I'm sorry, but I gotta go. She's waiting." And then, a little softer, she repeated, "I am sorry."

Sadly, without a word, Tuna reopened the blade and

*b*uurringg

ZAP!

the Starving Room was gone.

But even as she started toward her dresser to grab her bathing suit, TJ couldn't get the sound of the crying babies out of her head. She pretended not to be worried, but she was. Big-time. And the worrying that worried her worrier now was nothing compared to the worries that would soon worry her worrier even as she pretended not to worry.

TRANSLATION: ... (Never mind; you'll figure it out.)

CHAPTER FIVE

Amped-up Ambitions

TIME TRAVEL LOG:

Malibu, California, October 20—supplemental

Begin Transmission:

Uh-oh . . .

End Transmission

Elizabeth fought to walk at Hesper's side as they wheeled her best friend since forever toward the ambulance.

"Look out; coming through!" the driver shouted.

"Please, folks, step aside!" his partner yelled.

It was another emergency. The type Hesper

Breakahart lived for. The type that always got her headlines from all the Hollywood gossip shows and magazines:

Teen Idol Rushed to Hospital!

TV Celeb Fights for Life!!

Star Barely Survives Milk-Carton Attack!!!

Of course it took half a dozen phone calls to make sure the TV crews and magazines would be there. And an extra hour for Hesper's hairstylist to wash and condition her hair, not to mention the makeup people who needed to pluck out that stray eyebrow (*gasp*) and putty over that one slightly-larger-than-average pore (*double gasp*) on her skin.

Once those vital necessities were taken care of, they allowed the attendants to wheel her outside, where the cameras flashed and the reporters shouted:

"Miss Breakahart, how are you feeling?"

"Miss Breakahart, are you suing the milk company?"

"Miss Breakahart, will you ever walk again?"

Hesper smiled bravely through her pain while making sure the cameras got her best side. (As if she had a bad side. I mean, come on, we are talking Hesper Breakahart.) Elizabeth and the rest of Hesper's posse pushed and shoved everyone, making sure they were photographed right alongside their best friend since forever.

But Elizabeth had more reasons than just wanting to be in the magazines.

—Only Elizabeth had noticed the new kid completely disappearing right after the attack of the milk carton.

—Only Elizabeth had seen the boy with the funny clothes crammed into the new kid's locker.

—Only Elizabeth realized the new kid was a witch or an intergalactic alien or both.

So, moving in nice and close, she leaned into Hesper's ear and whispered, "I've got it all figured out."

Hesper looked at her.

"How we can get even with the new kid," Elizabeth explained. "Tell your secretary I'll call the girl about doing your paper . . . and all your other schoolwork."

Hesper nodded.

"And tell your TV producer I'll need to borrow three or four cameras."

"You have a plan?" Hesper whispered as she smiled and gave a brave thumbs-up to one of the reporters.

"Oh yeah." Elizabeth smiled back. "I'm going to videotape her in the very act of doing her weird stuff."

"That's great," Hesper whispered. "But listen, um, uh, whatever your name is . . ."

Elizabeth smiled and leaned closer as a hundred cameras photographed their faces side by side. "Yes?"

More brave smiles and thumbs-up as Hesper hissed, "Quit hogging my photographs or I'll get off this gurney and kick your butt."

"Got it," Elizabeth said, still smiling and stepping back. "No problem."

And it wasn't a problem. Because as they loaded Hesper into the ambulance, Elizabeth knew that within 24 hours, not only would she expose the new kid for who (or what) she was, but the great Hesper Breakahart would finally remember her name.

* * * * *

Chad wasn't crazy about helping Doug Claudlooper with his invention again. It made no difference that Doug had completely reworked it and even given it a brand-new name:

The Friction-Reduction-Through-Vertical-Amplification Surfboard

(Okay, so it still needed work.)

The point is, the kid inventor really had his heart set on helping Chad win the surfing competition. And since Chad was such a nice guy, and since Doug never stopped begging (or *sniff-sniff*-ing—honestly, had the kid ever heard of allergy medicine?), Chad finally agreed. Only this time it would be in Doug's garage. Doug's garage, where it was nice and safe. Doug's garage, where there would be no water to drown in or space shuttles to crash into.

Naomi Simpletwirp was there too. And if you

couldn't tell by her high, nasal voice, you could tell
by the

Click-ing, Clack-ing,

and

Crunch-ing

of her breath mints. Naomi always chewed breath
mints . . . when she wasn't sucking on breath strips,
taking shots of breath spray, or guzzling mouthwash.
I guess you could say she had a fear of bad breath.
While most kids carry cell phones in their pockets,
Naomi carried a tube of toothpaste and a tooth-
brush (with a spare one in her backpack in case of
emergencies).

    She had joined them in Doug's garage for one
simple reason: Doug was a science whiz and Naomi
was an AV whiz, which of course could only mean
one thing—love at first

Sniff, sniff

snort

click, clack

Crunch

sight.

The two were definitely at the bottom of Malibu Junior High's food chain—or as Hesper liked to call them, "bottom-feeders." But it never really bothered them, because as computer geniuses, they knew they'd eventually rule the world. And it didn't bother Chad, either. The truth was he cared less and less about what Hesper thought these days. Oh, they were still boyfriend/girlfriend, but for some reason, he was thinking more and more about the new kid who had moved in next door.

"Is she okay?" he asked Doug and Naomi as they placed the surfboard in a giant tub of water.

"You mean TJ?" Naomi asked.

"Yeah," Chad said. "It seems like whenever I'm around her, she gets all quiet and stuff."

Naomi turned to him. "You don't know why she gets that way?"

Chad shook his head. "Does she have a learning disability?"

Naomi stared at him.

"I noticed it too," Doug said as he picked up the surfboard's remote control. "It's like she only gets that way with you."

"Yeah," Chad said, frowning. "Did I do something to make her mad?"

Naomi looked at them both. "You're kidding me, right?"

Chad stared at her.

Doug stared at her.

"Neither of you can figure out why she acts so weird around Chad?"

Chad blinked.

Doug blinked (and *sniff*-ed).

Naomi shook her head. "Boys," she muttered. "Talk about clueless." Before she could explain, the surfboard in the tub

beep-ed

Chad looked toward it. "What's that mean?"

"It means we're ready," Doug said.

Chad nodded. "And what exactly does *this* surf-board do?"

beep . . . . beep

Naomi explained, "It creates its own sheet of water underneath."

Doug continued. "So instead of air shooting out, it shoots a jet stream of water, once again reducing friction and *(sniff-sniff)* allowing you to do more maneuvers."

Chad frowned. "I don't know, guys. . . ."

**beep . . . . beep . .
. . . . beep**

"Don't know what?" Doug said, glancing at his remote control.

"It still feels like cheating."

**beep . . . . . . beep . . . . . .
beep . . . . . . beep**

"As I've explained before *(snort-snort)*, it's only cheating if you get caught."

Chad shook his head. "I don't think so. Cheating is cheating. It makes no difference—"

beep . . . beep . . . beep . . . beep . . . beep . . . beep

"Uh, should those beeps be coming so fast?" he asked.

Doug scowled at his remote control. "Not exactly."

beep beep beep beep beep beep beep beep beep

Naomi looked over Doug's shoulder at the controls. "One beep is good."

"Correct." Doug nodded as he started backing up toward the door.

beep beep beep beep beep beep beep beep beep

beep beep beep beep beep beep beep beep beep

"And more than one beep?" Chad asked, his concern growing.

"Not so good," Naomi said as she also started backing up.

"Especially when they come so quickly," Doug added.

beep beep beep beep beep beep beep beep beep

beep beep beep beep beep beep beep beep beep

beep beep beep beep beep beep beep beep beep

beep beep beep beep beep beep beep beep beep

"So what do we do?" Chad asked.

beep beep beep beep beep beep beep beep beep

*beep beep beep beep beep beep
beep beep beep*

*beep beep beep beep beep beep
beep beep beep*

*beep beep beep beep beep beep
beep beep beep*

*beep beep beep beep beep beep
beep beep beep*

*beep beep beep beep beep beep
beep beep beep*

"We have several options," Doug said. "But for now, I think the best one is . . ."

He looked at the remote control, then at Naomi.

*beep beep beep beep beep beep
beep beep beep*

*beep beep beep beep beep beep
beep beep beep*

beep beep beep beep beep beep
beep beep beep

beep beep beep beep beep beep
beep beep beep

beep beep beep beep beep beep
beep beep beep

beep beep beep beep beep beep
beep beep beep

beep beep beep beep beep beep
beep beep beep

beep beep beep beep beep beep
beep beep beep

beep beep beep beep beep beep
beep beep beep

beep beep beep beep beep beep
beep beep beep

beep beep beep beep beep beep beep beep beep

beep beep beep beep beep beep beep beep beep

beep beep beep beep beep beep beep beep beep

And then together—in perfect, two-part harmony—
they shouted,

"RUN!!!"

All three spun around and raced toward the door.

The good news was they got outside and Doug
quickly pulled the garage door shut.

The better news was as they stood outside catching their breath, the alarm started to

*beep . . . . beep . . . . .
. . . beep*

slow down.

Naomi and Chad traded looks.

"You think it's safe?" Naomi asked.
Doug paused to listen.

beep . . . . **bee**p

"Yeah." He nodded. "It's definitely run out of

beep

power."

All three let out a sigh of relief.

Doug reached for the garage door and raised it
back up. "That was close."

"I'll say," Naomi agreed.

But just as the door opened—

beep beep beep beep beep beep beep
beep beep beep beep beep beep beep
beep beep beep beep beep beep beep
beep beep beep beep beep beep beep
beep beep beep beep beep beep beep
beep beep beep beep beep beep beep
beep beep beep beep beep beep beep
beep beep beep beep beep beep beep

beep beep beep beep beep beep beep
beep beep beep beep beep beep beep
beep beep beep beep beep beep beep
beep beep beep beep beep beep beep
beep beep beep beep beep beep beep
beep beep beep beep beep beep beep
beep beep beep beep beep beep beep
beep beep beep beep beep beep beep
beep beep beep beep beep beep beep
beep beep beep beep beep beep beep
beep beep beep beep beep beep beep
beep beep beep beep beep beep beep
beep beep beep beep beep beep beep
beep beep beep beep beep beep beep
beep beep beep beep beep beep beep
beep beep beep beep beep beep beep
beep beep beep beep beep beep beep
beep beep beep beep beep beep beep
beep beep beep beep beep beep beep
beep beep beep beep beep beep beep
beep beep beep beep beep beep beep
beep beep beep beep beep beep beep
beep beep beep beep beep beep beep

beep *beep* beep *beep* beep *beep* beep
beep *beep* beep *beep* beep *beep* beep
beep *beep* beep *beep* beep *beep* beep
beep *beep* beep *beep* beep *beep* beep
beep *beep* beep *beep* beep *beep* beep
beep *beep* beep *beep* beep *beep* beep
beep *beep* beep *beep* beep *beep* beep
beep *beep* beep *beep* beep *beep* beep
beep *beep* beep *beep* beep *beep* beep
beep *beep* beep *beep* beep *beep* beep
beep *beep* beep *beep* beep *beep* beep
beep *beep* beep *beep* beep *beep* beep
beep *beep* beep *beep* beep *beep* beep
beep *beep* beep *beep* beep *beep* beep
beep *beep* beep *beep* beep *beep* beep
beep *beep* beep *beep* beep *beep* beep
beep *beep* beep *beep* beep *beep* beep
beep *beep* beep *beep* beep *beep* beep
beep *beep* beep *beep* beep *beep* beep
beep *beep* beep *beep* beep *beep* beep
beep *beep* beep *beep* beep *beep* beep
beep *beep* beep *beep* beep *beep* beep
beep *beep* beep *beep* beep *beep* beep

beep beep beep beep beep beep beep beep beep beep beep beep beep

"Look out! It's going to—"

No one knew if Doug ever finished shouting. It's hard hearing anyone shout when a gazillion gallons of water suddenly

Gush

straight at you. We're not talking some little trickle of water. We're talking some huge

whoOOOOOSHH...

tidal wave.

The wall of water swept them off their feet and sent them flying down the alley at just under the speed of sound. It was like they were shooting rapids in a mighty

splish-splash . . . cough
splish-splash . . . gag

river.

(Okay, another exaggeration—but they did get a little wet.)

(Actually, a *lot* wet.)

And there was one other sound. The sound of a very nice surfer guy getting his foot hurt in a very big

"Augh"

Let's try that again. The sound of a very nice surfer guy getting his foot hurt in a very big

"AUGH!"

(that's better)

way.

"What happened?" Doug shouted.

"Are you pain?" Naomi asked.

Chad clenched his teeth, trying not to yell. He tried to stand but fell back to the ground.

"Here, let me see." Doug knelt down and reached for Chad's foot. "It doesn't look too bad."

"Doug?" Chad said.

Doug unlaced Chad's shoe and carefully pulled it off. "Hm, I don't see anything."

"Doug?"

He pulled off Chad's sock. "Are you sure it's hurt, 'cause it looks perfectly normal to—"

"Say, Doug?"

"Yes, Chad?"

"It's the other foot."

"Oh, right." Doug reached for the other shoe. "I knew that."

"What do you think?" Naomi asked. "Is it sprained?"

Doug pulled off Chad's sock and stared. "I don't think so."

Chad leaned back and sighed in relief. "Good, 'cause I sure don't want to miss the surfing meet."

"It's definitely not sprained," Doug said. Then, touching Chad's foot and causing another

"AUGH!"

he added, "But broken? Oh yeah. Big-time."

CHAPTER SIX

Caffeine Jitters

TIME TRAVEL LOG:

Malibu, California, October 20—supplemental

Begin Transmission:

Subject again under secret surveillance. Tuna hates the taste of motor oil, and I'm not gonzoed about scraping paint off my eyelids.

End Transmission

TJ felt good hanging with little Dorie as they headed for the beach. Ever since they'd moved to Malibu, things had been crazy in a mental-hospital kinda way. Life out here was like a car with no brakes and the gas pedal stuck on Ultra-Blur. Oh, sure, TJ's dad tried to make quality "family time" but it was pretty impossible with

—DAD'S BUSY SCHEDULE (TJ still wasn't sure what he did for work. Is any kid completely sure?)

—VIOLET'S SCHOOL STUFF (Besides being the family Einstein, Little Miss Perfect had to be president of all the school clubs . . . including Overachievers Anonymous.)

—TJ'S TRIPS THROUGH INSANITY (A daily event now that she had 23rd-century goofballs as her tour guides.)

So by comparison, agreeing to take Dorie swimming was a good thing.

"Now remember," TJ said as they approached the beach, "it's not the same as swimming in the lakes back home."

"Uh-huh," Dorie said.

"Back home, there's no surf."

"Uh-huh."

"Back home, there's no undertow."

"Uh-huh."

"Back home, there's—"

"How come you keep calling back home 'back home'?" Dorie asked.

"What do you mean?"

"I mean, isn't this our home now?"

TJ pushed her hair behind her ears and finally sighed. "Yeah, I guess it is."

The truth was it would never be home. At least to TJ. Home meant friends she'd grown up with. Home meant people and places she knew. Home meant a mother who had not left them by dying of cancer.

That last thought made the back of TJ's throat ache—just like it did at least once a day, ever since the funeral.

As if reading her thoughts, Dorie reached up and took her hand. "Do you ever think about her?"

"Who?" TJ asked. Her voice was thick with emotion and she coughed to hide it.

"Mom."

"All the time."

"Me too."

TJ wasn't sure what to say. But she didn't have to worry—Dorie was a nonstop talking machine. "Sometimes when I wake up in the morning, I think she's still alive."

TJ nodded.

"And then I remember she isn't and I get this big weight on my chest. You ever get that?"

"Yeah." TJ took another breath and repeated, "All the time."

"Yeah," Dorie repeated more softly, "me too."

TJ turned, pretending to look out toward the beach so Dorie couldn't see the tears filling her eyes. She missed Mom more than anything. It was like a big, gaping hole in the middle of her heart. People said the pain would eventually go away, but she had her doubts. And even if the pain did, she knew the hole would never leave.

"Yahoo!" Dorie shouted as they arrived at the sand and she began kicking it. "We're here!"

Yes, they were. And if you couldn't tell by all the beautiful, tan bodies (guys and girls), you could tell by the way all those beautiful tan bodies were staring at TJ and Dorie. Well, not really TJ and Dorie. More like TJ. Well, not really TJ. More like TJ's bathing suit.

Her *one-piece* bathing suit.

Back home, lots of girls wore them. It was something called *modesty*.

But *modesty* did not seem to be a word they understood in Malibu, California. Running around half-naked (actually more than half-naked) was more their style. While wearing modest, one-

piece bathing suits was definitely not. It's hard
to explain exactly what TJ was feeling—unless,
of course:

> **1.** your parents have ever dropped you off in
> front of school driving their horse and buggy,
> **2.** you've ever given an oral book report in
> front of the class while wearing your old *Star Wars*
> pajamas that nobody knows you still have, or
> **3.** your mother has ever popped into a
> slumber party and shouted, "Dear, here's an
> extra pair of undies in case you have one of your
> accidents."

Fortunately TJ's cell phone rang. She dug into her
bag to find it, grateful for something to do.

She was not so grateful to hear who was at the
other end of the phone.

"JB, this is Elizabeth, Hesper's best friend since
forever." The girl's voice was barely above a whisper.
"We need to talk."

TJ glanced at Dorie, who was laying her towel on
the sand. "Uh, I'm a little busy right now."

"Oh, you're going to be *a lot* busy."

"Is this about Hesper's report?"

"For starters, yes."

TJ swallowed. "Listen, I've been giving that some thought. I don't think it's such a good idea."

"Meet me at the coffee shop."

TJ frowned. "What? When?"

"Now."

"I just told you, I'm—"

"I know how you got that book report you handed in," Elizabeth said.

TJ went cold. "What do you mean?"

"I also know how that boy got in your locker and how you poured milk all over Hesper, and how you suddenly vanished."

"I didn't—"

"The coffee shop. Fifteen minutes. Be there."

"But—"

The phone went dead.

"Hello?" TJ said. *"Hello?"*

"Who's that?" Dorie asked, squinting at her and shading her eyes from the sun.

TJ looked at her little sister as she thought.

Did Elizabeth really know what was going on?

Probably not.

But could TJ take the chance?

Probably not.

With a heavy sigh, TJ closed her phone and said, "Sorry, Squid."

"About what?"

"We'll have to go swimming another day."

"But . . ." There was a catch in Dorie's voice. "You promised."

"I know, I know, and I'm sorry."

"But—"

"Grab your towel. We'll go swimming tomorrow."

"You promise?"

"Yeah, yeah, I promise," TJ said. "Now let's get you home."

* * * * *

Little Dorie was anything but thrilled. Not that TJ blamed her. After all, she *had* promised. In a way, Tuna and Herby were right. Cheating did have its consequences. And you didn't have to travel into the future to see them. All you had to do was look at the disappointed face of one six-year-old sister.

But TJ had to see what Elizabeth knew—or pretended she knew. After that, she was certain things would finally settle down. At least that's what she told herself as she opened the door to the coffee shop.

It was a pretty cool place, and it was swarming with kids. The line stretched forever. It was like her whole generation was hooked on coffee. Some even shuffled along the hallways at school with bottles of it attached to hospital IV drip stands.

(All right, another exaggeration. But not as bad as . . .)

And the kids seemed to get younger all the time. Rumor had it, some mothers were even slipping coffee into their baby's bottles.

(I told you.)

What wasn't an exaggeration was having to pay $5.95 for a small coffee with a bunch of whipped cream on it. Well, that's what others paid. To be honest, TJ didn't have that kind of money. To be hon-ester (don't try that word on your English teacher) she hated the taste: burnt and bitter. Yes, sir, how could anyone pass up paying a fortune for that?

It wasn't hard spotting Elizabeth sitting off in the corner. There was something about the orange cover-alls, black rubber boots, and white surgical gloves that gave her away. And if that didn't do it, there was always the bee hat with the net draped over her face. Or the smell of garlic coming from a garlic bulb necklace hanging around her neck.

"Elizabeth?" TJ asked as she approached.

"Stay back."

TJ came to a stop.

"The Internet says witches can't work their magic if we're over six feet away from them."

"All right . . . ," TJ said slowly. She reached for a chair and pulled it from the table to sit.

As she did, Elizabeth produced a giant cross from her pocket and held it toward TJ . . . just to be safe.

TJ frowned. "Isn't that supposed to be for vampires? And what's with the bee mask?"

"It protects me from deadly photon rays that shoot from the eyes of outer-space aliens."

Cautiously, TJ eased herself into the chair. "I'm confused. What do you think I am? A vampire, a witch, or an alien?"

"Maybe all three," Elizabeth said as she pulled a bottle of holy oil from her pocket and poured it on the table between them. "The point is to stop you from reaching me with your superhuman powers."

TJ tried not to laugh. "What about the kryptonite? You forgot the kryptonite."

"It's in the mail."

TJ could only shake her head in amazement. She glanced around the coffee shop, noticing the portrait of Mrs. May K. Buck, the owner, that hung behind the counter. It was your average, run-of-the-mill painting of some average, run-of-the-mill lady. What was not so average and run-of-the-mill were her eyes.

Eyes that were shifting from side to side. Eyes that just happened to look like they belonged to . . .

"*Herby!*" TJ hissed.

The eyes blinked.

"What did you say?" Elizabeth asked.

TJ gave Herby another glare before turning back to Elizabeth and trying to smile. "Nothing; nothing at all. What were you saying?"

Elizabeth looked at her skeptically. "I'm saying I know you're not human. And if you don't write Hesper Breakahart's history report, I'll expose you to the whole world."

TJ stole another look at Herby, who blinked and scowled. But she didn't need his help to say no. She turned back to Elizabeth and said, "I told you, I don't think that's such a good idea."

"Why, because you want someone else to have a better report?" She looked around and lowered her voice. "Haven't you learned by now that Hesper always has to have the biggest and best of everything?"

"No, that's not it," TJ said.

"Then what?"

TJ hesitated, then explained, "It's cheating."

"So? Everybody cheats."

TJ took a breath. She had a point. It seemed

everyone cheated. And not just kids. Grown-ups, too. Businessmen, lawyers, movie stars, politicians. Everybody. And if doing it just one more time would keep Elizabeth from blabbing whatever she thought she knew to the rest of the world . . .

TJ glanced back to the portrait of Mrs. May K. Buck, whose eyebrows were now pointed down in a scowl. TJ looked away, out the window into the parking lot.

Elizabeth continued. "If you don't do Hesper's history report and if you don't make it the biggest and best ever written, I will totally expose you."

"Expose me as what? How?"

"Oh, we've got our ways." Elizabeth nodded. "Believe me, we've got our ways."

It was TJ's turn to scowl. The girl still hadn't said anything about Tuna or Herby. Maybe she was just bluffing. Then again, Elizabeth had seen the boy in her locker, she had seen the milk pouring over Hesper's head, and she had seen TJ's vanishing act in the cafeteria.

Maybe cheating just one last time wouldn't be so bad.

"So," TJ said, "if I write this one report for Hesper, you'll leave me alone?"

"Completely. No questions asked."

"Forever?"

"Forever."

"And you won't tell anyone?"

"Not a soul."

TJ hesitated. It was a pretty sweet deal. And if she could get Herby and Tuna to do the report for her, like they did her book report, well, it would be even sweeter.

"What do you say?" Elizabeth asked.

TJ was about to answer when, suddenly, a car alarm to a Ford pickup

waaa-ooo . . . waaa-ooo . . . waaa-ooo

went off in the parking lot . . . along with its flashing lights. It wasn't a big deal. It happened all the time. What *was* a big deal was the lights were not the lights to a Ford pickup. They were *Tuna's eyes*, which kept opening and closing, opening and closing!

"TUNA?!" TJ cried out.

waaa-ooo . . . waaa-ooo . . . waaa-ooo

"What did you say?" Elizabeth shouted over the alarm.

TJ didn't know whether to

A) Be frightened
B) Be surprised
C) Be angry
D) Be all of the above

Unfortunately, she chose D.

"TUNA!" Rising from her chair, she raced through the crowded coffee shop and out into the parking lot.

Elizabeth followed right on her heels (while staying at least six feet away and holding out her cross). "What's going on?" she shouted. "Is the mother ship trying to contact you?"

"It's nothing!" TJ yelled. "Absolutely nothing!"

"Are you sure?" Elizabeth shouted.

"I'm sure."

"Then why is it doing that?"

TJ turned to see Tuna (aka a Ford pickup) not only

waaa-ooo . . . waaa-ooo . . . waaa-ooo-ing

but beginning to

bounce . . . bounce . . . bounce

like a pogo stick after one too many cups of Mrs. May K. Buck's brew.

Of course this made TJ even angrier. How dare the boys do this to her! Didn't they trust her?

"What's wrong with it?" Elizabeth shouted.

TJ spun back to her and yelled, "How should I know? It's just some stupid truck with some stupid short in the alarm. Listen, about doing that history report for Hesper?"

"Yeah?"

"I'd be happy to!" TJ yelled nice and loud, making sure Tuna could hear her over the honking. "In fact, I'll make it the best report the whole school has ever seen!"

As soon as the words came out of her mouth, Herby and Tuna both

krinkle . . . krackle

POOF!

morphed beside her, and the car alarm abruptly
came to a

waaa-Ooo . . . Waaa-

stop. (It's hard to keep a car alarm going when
there's no longer a car.)

"What do you think you're doing!?" she shouted
at Herby.

He shrugged.

"Tuna?!"

Without a word, Tuna opened the blade to their
Swiss Army Knife and they were

chugga-chugga-chugga

BLING!

transported back to TJ's house.

That was the good news.

The bad news was she'd have a little more
explaining to do about why she, a Ford pickup, and
a portrait of Mrs. May K. Buck had all vanished from
the coffee shop.

CHAPTER SEVEN

A Not-So-Bright Future

TIME TRAVEL LOG:

Malibu, California, October 20—supplemental

Begin Transmission:
More glimpses into future. Subject still unable to
see what huge zworkedness comes from a little
torkedness.

End Transmission

"Why do you keep spying on me?" TJ demanded
once she and the boys were back in her room.

"Why do you keep thinking of cheating?" Tuna
asked.

TJ felt her face growing hot with anger. "*You're* the ones who started this."

"And you are the one who can stop it."

"By confessing to Miss Grumpaton and getting an F in English?!"

"An F in English is better than an F in life."

TJ put her hands on her hips. "What's that supposed to mean?"

As an answer, Tuna reached for his Swiss Army Knife and pulled out another blade.

"Oh no," TJ moaned, "not

buurringg

ZAP!

again."

Of course there had been the usual flash of light, and of course they were surrounded by the usual holograph of the future . . . except this particular future looked exactly like the present. Same bedroom. Same boxes she *still* hadn't unpacked since moving. (She's a bit of a slob.)

"What's going on?" TJ asked. "Where are we?"

"Five years into the future," Tuna said.

(Okay, she's a *huge* slob.)

Herby motioned across the room to her desk. It was covered in a mountain of papers. TJ frowned and stepped closer until she spotted an older version of herself behind the papers. She was hunched over the desk, furiously typing away. She was about 18 and anything but pretty. (Unless by *pretty* you mean bloodshot eyes, ratty hair that hadn't been brushed in a month, and teeth that hadn't been brushed in longer than that.)

Then there was the shaking. Her whole body trembled, and her face twitched nervously.

TJ turned to the boys, waiting for an explanation.

Herby cleared his throat. "When Your Dude-ness agreed to cheat for Hesper, the word spread. Soon other students asked for your help."

"Why didn't I say no?" TJ asked.

Tuna opened another blade and

RIIIIIIIIIP . . .

the room was suddenly split into two. On one side sat the exhausted, overworked TJ in her sloppy bedroom. On the other side sat Elizabeth, talking on the phone in her super-rich, has-everything-a-person-could-ever-want bedroom.

"Don't worry," Elizabeth was saying. "She'll have a term paper to you by Friday. And at $20 a page times 100 pages, that comes to—" She reached for a calculator and started adding.

TJ asked, "She's making me do other people's papers?"

Herby nodded. "She kept threatening to tell on you if you didn't do more papers for more people. Pretty soon, she had you slaving away night and day."

"That's terrible," TJ exclaimed.

"For you, yes," Tuna agreed. "But for her it became quite a moneymaking business."

"Why am I shaking like that?"

"You had to stay awake, so you became a caffeine addict," Tuna said. "Waaay too much coffee."

"But I don't like the taste of coffee."

"You won't be tasting it," Tuna said.

TJ turned to him as he strolled over to the desk. He pushed aside the papers so she could get a better look. That's when she gasped. (Remember the exaggeration about kids getting their coffee through hospital IV stands? Well, for the future TJ, it wasn't an exaggeration.)

She couldn't believe her eyes. "That's terrible!"

Herby nodded. "Zworked to the max."

"But once I graduate . . . I mean, after that, everything will be all right. Right?"

The boys traded looks.

"Right?" TJ repeated.

Without a word, Tuna reached for his knife.

TJ groaned. "Oh

buurringgg

ZAP!

no."

Now they stood in a huge, messy office. On the far wall was a giant screen with a 30-year-old version of Hesper Breakahart. She was yelling at an older version of TJ, who was even skinnier than before. Her ratty hair (which hadn't been brushed since the last time) was already turning gray. A cigarette dangled from her mouth, and she was shaking worse than ever.

"I don't have enough lines!" Hesper was screaming.

"I gave you every line in the scene," TJ said as she reached into her desk drawer and pulled out a bottle of antacids.

"Well, I want more!"

"Yes, Ms. Breakahart," TJ said, shaking out a handful of the tablets.

"Get rid of all the other actors! Just have me talking to myself!"

"Yes, Ms. Breakahart." TJ threw the antacids into her mouth and began chewing them.

"In fact, have three of me talking to me! That way I'll get three times the lines!"

"Excellent point, Ms. Breakahart," TJ said and went back to typing.

"And I need them now!"

"Yes, Ms. Breakahart."

TJ turned to Tuna, who explained, "You wrote so many reports for Hesper that she made you the head writer of her TV show."

"But I don't want to be a writer."

Tuna shook his head. "It doesn't matter. With Elizabeth at her side, you had no choice."

TJ moved closer to her older self and watched with pity as the woman kept typing, smoking, and chewing antacids.

"What about all that caffeine?" TJ asked. "And the smoking? Don't I know that will kill me?"

"It's the only way you thought you could keep going," Herby said.

TJ felt a knot forming in her gut. Finally she looked back to the boys. "But I quit, don't I? I mean, I eventually find a way out and quit, right?"

Tuna and Herby traded looks.

"Guys?"

More looking.

"Guys, answer me!"

Reluctantly, Tuna reached for the blade and

buurringg

ZAP!

they were standing with the rest of her family at an outdoor get-together. There were cousins and aunts from all over the country. But they were all dressed up . . . and crying.

"Oh, TJ . . . ," her dad moaned.

She turned to see him. He was wearing his suit and looked a thousand years older than she remembered. On one side of him stood an older version of Violet. On the other was little Dorie, all grown-up.

"It's okay, Daddy." Dorie's voice was hoarse from crying. She held Dad's arm, trying to comfort him.

He nodded, blinking his eyes. But it did no good. The tears began to fall.

Violet took his other arm and croaked, "She's a lot happier where she is now."

TJ turned to Tuna and Herby. "Who are they talking about?" she asked—though she already had a sneaking suspicion. "And where am I? I see Dad. I see Dorie and Violet. Where am I?"

Neither boy answered (unless you count their own sniffing and eye wiping an answer).

"Guys?" she demanded.

At last Herby motioned behind her.

TJ turned completely around to see . . . a casket suspended over an open grave.

She sucked in her breath. "That's . . . me?"

Tuna nodded.

"H-how?" she stuttered. "What happened?"

"You worked too hard," Tuna said. "All that caffeine, all those cigarettes, the stress . . . it was more than your heart could—"

"Oh, TJ!" Suddenly Dad threw himself over the casket. He began to sob uncontrollably. "TJ, don't leave me, please . . ."

Others in the group also began to cry. Dorie stepped up to join Dad. She wrapped her arms around him, trying to pull him away. "It's okay, Daddy," she choked through her own tears. "Daddy, don't cry. Please don't cry. . . ."

"Dad," TJ called out, tears filling her own eyes. She tried to reach out and touch him. But since he was a holographic image, her hand passed right through. "I'm here, Dad. I'm right beside you. . . ."

"He can't hear you," Herby said.

"It's just a projected image," Tuna reminded her.

"But . . ." She turned to them. They looked all blurry through her tears. "It doesn't have to be this way, right?"

Herby glanced nervously to Tuna.

"Right?" she repeated. "This is just one possibility. Right? *Right?*"

"If you decide to cheat for Hesper . . ." Tuna dropped off, unable to continue.

"What?" TJ choked, wiping her face. "What?!"

"If you decide to cheat for Hesper, this is your *only* future."

TJ turned back to her father, tears streaming down her own face.

"Dude," Herby whispered to Tuna, "I think we better go."

Tuna nodded.

"No, I want to stay." TJ wiped her eyes. "There's got to be some way to let him know!"

Tuna reached for the knife blade. "We have to go."

"NO!" TJ shouted. "I want to talk to him. I want him to see that everything will be all—"

buurringgg

ZAP!

Suddenly the three of them were back in her room.

CHAPTER EIGHT

Stranger than Fiction . . . or Not.

TIME TRAVEL LOG:
Malibu, California, October 21

Begin Transmission:
Subject begins seeing how zworked cheating is.
Hope it's not too late.

End Transmission

Chad Steel hobbled into Miss Grumpaton's English class on his crutches. Of course all the girls *ooh*-ed and *aah*-ed in sympathy . . . and of course all the guys asked if they could break his other leg so he wouldn't walk lopsided.

(Sometimes guys aren't great at showing sympathy.)

"There's an empty seat up front here," Miss Grumpaton said. "Sit there next to Thelma Jean so you don't have so far to walk."

Chad threw a look to the back of the class, where Hesper sat holding court. (Wherever Hesper sat, she held court.) He knew she wouldn't be thrilled about his sitting so far away. Then again, she was so busy being the center of attention, it was doubtful she'd notice. So far she'd not even noticed his broken leg.

(Sometimes princesses aren't so good at showing sympathy either.)

He laid his crutches against the front desk, glanced at the new kid, and smiled. "Hey," he said.

She muttered something that might have been "Hey," then quickly looked the other direction, tugging at her hair.

Chad stood staring a moment. Once again he tried figuring out what he'd done to make her so mad. And once again he wondered how he could apologize if she never talked to him.

Girls. Go *figure.*

With a sigh, he eased himself into the seat. The bell rang and Miss Grumpaton began her nonstop lecture on whatever she was nonstop lecturing about.

Chad tried to pay attention, but his thoughts were still on Sunday's surfing meet. The meet he could no longer compete in because of his broken foot. Actually, he could compete—there was no rule about surfing with a cast on. They just frowned on their contestants drowning. And that's exactly what would happen to Chad. Unless . . .

His mind drifted back to Doug's promise:

"With my new and improved surfboard (sniff-sniff), *you can win even wearing a cast!"*

"But wouldn't that still be cheating?" Chad had argued.

"I keep telling you (snort-snort), *it's only cheating if you get caught."*

Chad knew Doug was wrong. But he also knew there was no way he could compete if he didn't go along with Doug's plan.

He glanced at TJ. She was shifting and fidgeting in a major sort of way. At first he thought it was because she hated sitting so close to him . . . until he turned his attention back to Miss Grumpaton's speech.

". . . is an example of what you all can do if you put your mind to it." She looked directly at TJ and smiled. "Thelma Jean, I don't know what they taught you back in Minnesota, but I think we could all learn a lesson about what hard work can accomplish. Isn't that right, class?"

The class gave their the usual response of gum

Snap-snap-*Snap*-ing

text message

click-*click*-click-ing

and cell phone

ring-*ring*-ring-ing

But Miss Grumpaton was a pro. She could keep boring you no matter what you did.

"And you'll all be happy to know that I've submitted Thelma Jean's name to participate in a national essay contest. Isn't that exciting?"

Chad stole another look at TJ . . . who was slowly melting into her seat.

"Thelma Jean will be representing our school nationally. And if she does well, as I'm sure she will—" Miss Grumpaton paused to give one of her famous yellow-from-way-too-many-cups-of-tea grins—"she will go on to represent us internationally. Isn't that simply thrilling?"

Snap-snap-snap

Click-click-click

Heavy metal ring tone here . . .

Michael Jackson ring tone there . . .

"However, there is just one problem." Miss Grumpaton turned her smile back on TJ, who was doing her best imitation of the Wicked-Witch-of-the-West-meets-water. "The essay is due Monday. Though I'm sure that won't be a problem for you, will it, Thelma Jean?"

Chad could practically hear TJ crying, *"I'm melting . . . I'm melting."*

Then, before anyone broke into a chorus of "Ding-Dong! The Witch Is Dead," the classroom door flew open. There, before them, stood some pirate guy with a peg leg, who was shouting, "Argh!" On his shoulder he had a parrot that screeched, **"Pieces of eight! Pieces of eight!"**

Of course the class gasped. And of course, Miss Grumpaton demanded, "Do you have a hall pass?"

The pirate gave another "Argh!" then

step-clomp, step-clomp-ed

toward the teacher, shouting, "Where's me treasure map?"

"You mean, 'Where's *my* treasure map,'" Miss Grumpaton corrected. "The use of a possessive pronoun in the sentence is necessary in order to—"

"Silence, woman!"

Miss Grumpaton shook her head. "If you are to remain in my class, you must learn the proper use of grammar."

Without a word, he pulled an old-fashioned pistol from his belt.

More class gasping.

And more bird screeching, **"Shiver me timbers! Shiver me timbers!"**

But no more Miss Grumpaton lecturing . . . at least for the moment. Instead, to everyone's astonishment, she started to giggle.

Chad looked on. He'd never seen an English

teacher lose her mind before . . . but there was a first time for everything.

The pirate waved his gun at her. "Ye think this be funny?"

"Pieces of eight! Pieces of eight!"

Miss Grumpaton's giggles grew into laughter.

"Stow that caterwauling!"

But her laughter only increased until she could barely catch her breath. "Oh, gracious," she said, wiping the tears from her eyes. "You are good."

The pirate, who was used to being taken a bit more seriously, especially when holding a loaded gun, made his move. He quickly stepped behind her and wrapped his arm around her neck, holding the pistol to her head.

"Oh, this is good," Miss Grumpaton laughed. "Whoever thought this up gets an A+ for extra credit."

"Silence, or be ye keelhauled!" the pirate shouted.

"And so authentic." She frowned, waving her hands in front of her nose. "Though I could do without the fake smell of rum on your breath!"

The pirate cocked his pistol. "If ye don't be silent, I shall send ye to Davy Jones's locker!"

Chad watched the performance with the rest of

the class. At least he *thought* it was a performance (though the pirate was nowhere near as realistic as in the movies).

To his surprise, TJ leaped to her feet and shouted, "Stop it!" She looked around the room as if searching for somebody. "Herby! Tuna! Stop it this instant!"

"Thelma Jean!" Miss Grumpaton laughed. "Is this your doing? I might have guessed!"

TJ continued searching the room and yelling, "Make him go!"

There was no answer except . . .

—Miss Grumpaton's laughing
—the pirate's *argh!*-ing
—the parrot's **Pieces of eight! Pieces of eight!**-ing.

Suddenly the pirate's eyes widened. "Shiver me timbers!" he shouted at TJ. "I've seen ye before."

"Actually, that's 'Shiver *my* timbers,'" Miss Grumpaton corrected. "Once again, the use of a possessive pronoun is mandatory if—"

The pirate tossed her to the side and, in one swift move, lunged for the girl. TJ turned to run, but he caught her arm.

"Let me go!" she screamed.

"Ye be the cause of all this, missy?" he shouted.

"Let me go! Let me go!"

"Jim Hawkins, me cabin boy—he's seen ye too!"

"Oh, this is good," Miss Grumpaton exclaimed. "Class, I hope you're taking notes."

"Let me go!" TJ cried. "You're hurting me!"

Acting or no acting, Chad had seen enough. There was something about the pain in TJ's voice . . . and the fear in her eyes. Without stopping to think, he leaped at the pirate from his desk.

Unfortunately, his leaper was a little lame. (Having a cast on your foot tends to do that.) So instead of grabbing the pirate and freeing TJ, Chad sort of stumbled and fell into the man, causing

> —the parrot to fly off, screeching
> —the pirate to fall back, cursing
> —Chad to fall on him, *ooaff!*-ing
> —the pistol to hit the ground, *k-blewie*-ing

which caused

> —the class to drop to the floor, screaming
> —Miss Grumpaton to stand there, laughing
> —TJ to keep on yelling

Chad and the pirate began wrestling on the floor

roll, roll, roll-ing

this way. And

roll, roll, roll-ing

that way, until . . .

zibwa-zibwa-zibwa

DING!

Chad was suddenly

roll, roll, roll-ing

by himself. Talk about weird. One minute he held the pirate in his hands. The next he held only air. He looked around, blinking, then slowly sat up.

Students began climbing back into their seats. Some were crying; others were sobbing. TJ was still standing, looking all around. And Miss Grumpaton?

She started to clap.

"Excellent, my dear!" she said. "I don't know how you did it, but your extra credit report was superb!" Then, turning to the class, she said, "And that, boys and girls, is why she will do so well in writing her essay this weekend. Imagination, creativity, and all of that hard work will someday make her a great writer!"

* * * * *

It was Friday night, which meant another one of Dad's attempts at *Hey let's have some quality family time and go out for pizza.*

(Good ol' Dad, he just doesn't give up.)

Of course Dorie was all for it. Dorie was all for everything—give her a fingernail clipping and she'll play with it for hours.

But Violet (who's never all for anything) had her usual *I'm a health nut so everyone has to suffer because of me* conditions. "I'll go," she said, "but only if no animals were hurt in the making of the food substance—"

TRANSLATION: *Kiss the pepperoni good-bye.*

AAAARGH!!!

"and there are no dairy products used—"

TRANSLATION: *Kiss the cheese good-bye.*

"and no chemicals or artificial flavors are added."

TRANSLATION: *Kiss the taste good-bye.*
(Unless you wanted to eat the box, which ALWAYS had more flavor than the pizzas she ordered.)

But as exciting as it all sounded, TJ decided to pass.

Dad was disappointed, and Dorie begged her to come (and Violet asked if she could have her extra pieces). But TJ had more important things on her mind. She had to make a decision.

And the best place for making important decisions was where she was now . . . walking alone on the beach at sunset.

It was hard to believe that one little bit of cheating could cause so many problems. It seemed like every time she turned around, it got worse. And this time it had nothing to do with Tuna and Herby's attempts at spying or their trips into her future or their fritzing Swiss Army Knife.

Instead, it had everything to do with Hesper

expecting her to write her history report, Elizabeth threatening to tell the school she was some strange weirdo (as if they didn't already know), and Miss Grumpaton expecting her to write some amazing essay for some national contest.

Maybe Tuna and Herby were right. Maybe she should put a stop to it. Maybe she should tell Miss Grumpaton that she cheated. Sure, it would mean getting an F, but at least things would get back to normal (well, as normal as possible with two boys from the 23rd century haunting her life).

Maybe the old saying really was true. Maybe honesty really was the best policy.

These were the thoughts spinning through TJ's brain until she looked down at the sand and froze. Because there, with everybody else's footprints, were holes spaced evenly apart.

Holes that could only be made by someone with a peg leg!

Or . . .

"Hey."

She looked up and was startled to see Chad Steel just ahead. He was walking on the beach with his crutches. Immediately, her hand shot up to her hair to smooth it . . . or cover her face . . . or both. There was also the sudden pounding of her heart, so loud she barely heard her own voice croak back, "Hi."

He waited for her to catch up. She ordered her legs to move and someway—she wasn't sure how—they obeyed. A moment later they were walking side by side.

After a few seconds of deathly silence (which felt more like years of deathly silence), Chad finally cleared his throat. "That was something today in English class, wasn't it?"

"Uh-huh."

More deathly silence.

He tried again. "I mean, whoever that actor was, he was good."

"Uh-huh."

Repeat in the deathly silence department.

"Talk about a fast exit. It was like he disappeared right out of my hands."

"Uh-huh." TJ was sure she knew other words, but at the moment she couldn't think of any.

He turned to look at the sun setting over the water. Purple and pink bands spread across the sky, so vivid it was like it was on fire. "Sure is pretty," he said.

All right, it was now or never. She would go out on a limb. She would say something deep and profound. Something that would impress this incredible guy with her incredible intelligence. Taking a deep breath for courage, she went for broke and croaked, "Yeah."

(So much for incredible intelligence.)

They continued down the beach.

Once again he tried to make conversation. "I come here this time of night when I have things to work out."

She turned to him, amazed. Of course she wanted to tell him that's exactly why she was there. Unfortunately, that would involve opening her mouth and sounding like a human being, which she knew was out of the question, so she let him continue.

"Doug Claudlooper has been building this fancy surfboard that he wants me to use in Sunday's competition."

TJ returned to her old habits. "Uh-huh." (Better safe than sorry.)

"I mean, it's supposed to help me win and everything—even with this stupid cast, which no one would notice under my wet suit."

"Uh-huh."

"But using a nonregulation board is definitely cheating, and I just don't know if I want to do that."

If TJ's jaw had dropped any lower, it would have hit the sand. Was it possible? He was struggling with the very thing she was! Unbelievable. Here she was, feeling so alone and cut off, absolutely positive that nobody would understand what she was going through . . . and then, out of the blue, this incredible guy showed up and said he was fighting exactly the same thing. Amazing. She *wasn't* alone. She wanted to say all this and more, but her throat was already closing up with emotion. She cleared it and tried to speak, to blurt out all these feelings and more, but of course nothing came . . . unless you count tears filling her eyes.

Tears?! she thought. *Oh, brother, what's that about?* She turned her head. If she was lucky, he wouldn't see them. (Then again, we all know about her luck.)

"Hey, you okay?" he asked.

She angrily swiped at her eyes.

"Are you crying?"

She shook her head, refusing to look at him.

"You are, aren't you? What did I say this time?"

And then, before she could stop herself, she turned and bolted away. She wasn't sure why. All she knew was she had to get away before he thought she was a total mental case—which, she figured, he might already suspect.

"Hey!" he shouted.

But TJ didn't turn back. She just kept running.

"I'm sorry!"

Tears spilled onto her cheeks and ran down her face.

"Whatever I said, I'm really, really sorry!"

She didn't answer, just kept running.

CHAPTER NINE

Hide and Go EEEK!

Malibu, California, October 21—supplemental

Begin Transmission:

*Uninvited guest dropped by. Subject not home, so
we entertained. Had great time—except for the
ghosts.*

End Transmission

As TJ was busy having her little meltdown with
Chad, Elizabeth was having her little break-in at TJ's.

Actually, it was pretty easy to break in through
TJ's bathroom window. Her dad always left it open

because he figured no one was small enough to climb in. Normally, he'd be right. But he'd forgotten they now lived in . . .

Malibu, California—the stick-figure capital of the world.

Malibu, California—where everyone tries to imitate the walking skeletons they see in fashion magazines.

Malibu, California—where every sickly-looking, starving girl starves herself so she could look like every other sickly-looking, starving girl.

So, needless to say, it was a breeze for Elizabeth to slip in through the window. Once inside, she began pulling out the tiny surveillance cameras Hesper's TV producer had loaned her. They were barely the size of a pack of gum, which made Elizabeth's plan all the easier. She'd simply stick them up around the house, turn them on by remote control, and record TJ casting spells, doing voodoo, or communicating with the mother ship.

And once she had the proof on tape, she could force TJ to do whatever she wanted for as long as she wanted.

The plan was flawless . . . except for the strange

and creepy voices she heard as she entered the
upstairs hallway.

"*Zwork!*" a voice whispered from behind her.
"*What's she doing here?*"

Elizabeth gasped and spun around. But nobody
was there.

"*It's Hesper's best friend,*" another voice whispered.
"*The one since forever.*"

Again Elizabeth spun around. And again it
was nobody. And seeing two nobodies meant
the same as seeing no nobodies, which meant
that the nobodies really had no bodies and were
actually . . .

"GHOSTS!" Elizabeth screamed.

"*WHERE?*" the first voice screamed back.

"*HIDE ME!*" the second voice cried.

But Elizabeth was in no mood for a conversation . . . especially with two nobodies who had no
bodies who . . . Let's not do that again. Instead,
let's just say she had three choices:

A) Scream and faint in fear
B) Run for her life
C) Escape into the nearest room

The good news was she chose C (and a little bit of A, so she could still work in the screaming).

The bad news was the nearest room was TJ's.

Elizabeth raced into the darkened room and slammed the door behind her.

Everything was very quiet and very still . . . except for the voices whispering right beside her.

"Are they gone?"

"Who?"

"The ghosts!"

Elizabeth caught her breath, trying not to scream.

"How should I know? I can't see a thing. Turn on the light."

Elizabeth's heart raced as the lights blazed on. Frantically, she looked about the room, but no one was there. She took a deep breath for courage and then another. Finally she called out, "Who . . . who's there? Who are you? What's going on?"

"How are we going to get her out of here?"

"Good question."

Elizabeth tried to swallow. "I . . . I'm not going anywhere."

"Perhaps the Reverse Beam Blade?"

"Good thinking."

"Who are you?" Elizabeth took a step forward. "What planet do you—?"

Raaaapha . . .
Reeeepha . . . Riiiipha . . .

BOING-oing-OING-oing-oing!

Suddenly Elizabeth felt her body spinning around and her feet walking. But they weren't walking forward. They were walking backward. In fact, everything about her was moving backward. Including her words:

"?—uoy od tenalp tahW ?uoy era ohW"

No matter how hard she tried to walk and talk normally, she couldn't.

".erehwyna gniog ton m'I . . . I"

She continued backward toward the door exactly as she had entered. Except for one minor detail.

"She's off angle, dude."

"What?"

"She's going to miss the doorway; she's going to hit the wall."

And that's exactly what she did. But instead of hitting the wall and stopping, she kept right on going . . . right up the wall.

"?
n
o

g
n
i
o
g

s'
t
a
h
W"

"Turn it off, Herby. Bring her back down."
"I'm trying."

Along with the voices, Elizabeth heard a strange

thwack, *thwack* **thwack-**ing

followed by more

Raaaapha . . .
Reeeepha . . . Riiiipha . . .

which ended in a pathetic little

BLAAHHHhhh . . .

Unfortunately, her human fly routine wasn't quite over. Because once she reached the ceiling, she took another corner and started upside down across it.

"Ʒuoy era ohW Ʒereht

s'
o
h
w
. . .
o
h
W"

Elizabeth was definitely not having a good time. In fact, she was trying really hard to pass out, but it's hard passing out when you're standing upside down and all the blood is rushing to your head.

Fortunately, after a few more

thwack, thwack, thwacks

and one or two more

Raaaapha . . .
Reeeepha . . . Riiiipha . . .

BLAAHHHhhhs

she finally heard a slightly reassuring sound.

Raaaapha . . .
Reeeepha . . . Riiiipha . . .

BOING-oing-oing-oing-oing!

And just like that, she

"
A
u
g
h
h
!
"

fell to the

T H u d

floor.

Needless to say, she felt great being on the ground again. But this was no time to stick around and celebrate. It was, however, a time to run out of the room, stumble down the stairs, and race outside.

It was also a time to bump into TJ, who was
coming back from the beach, and to scream to
her, "PLEASE! I promise I won't tell anyone! Just
don't kidnap me to your planet or turn me into
a toad!"

And with that friendly farewell, Elizabeth turned
and continued running for her life.

* * * * *

The following morning, bright and early, Chad was
out on his surfboard. He'd made his decision . . .
or Doug had worn him down until he'd made it.
There's something about 2:00 a.m. calls that can do
that. . . .

And if 2:00 a.m. calls don't work, there's always
2:49 a.m. calls,
3:10 a.m. calls,
3:51 a.m. calls,
4:07 a.m. calls,
4:45 a.m. calls,
5:06 a.m. calls,

and . . . well, let's just say Doug can be pretty persistent.

By 7:12 a.m., Chad had finally agreed to try
out the new board. Unfortunately, all the listening

to Doug's talking (and *sniff-sniff*-ing) had worn him out. He was so tired, he could barely stand. But it didn't matter. Once they sealed his cast in a giant plastic bag and put on his wet suit, everything was automatic. All Chad had to do was stand up (with the help of a metal brace running down his legs and powerful magnets attached to the board) and let Doug do all the work.

It was beautiful.

Well, it was beautiful after the first thermonuclear explosion, the six trips to the ER, and a visit by the USS *Kitty Hawk* to stop what they thought was a national invasion.

(Okay, that's another exaggeration—there were only *three* trips to the ER.)

Anyway, by the end of the day, all of the kinks were worked out. There was little doubt that tomorrow Chad Steel would be able to shut down all the competition and become a major winner. Now, if he could just shut down all the guilty thoughts that said he was a major loser. Actually, his thoughts weren't really calling him a loser. They were calling him something else. A word starting with $C H E A$, ending in $T E R$, and without many letters in between.

AAAARGH!!!

* * * * *

TJ's Saturday was about the same as Chad's . . . but without the cool beach, beautiful ocean, or occasional visit by aircraft carriers.

However, she did have plenty of crumpled papers to keep her company, since crumpled papers are what you get when you try 2,121 times to start an essay that you're clueless about how to write. That's right; she'd also given in to the dark side in a major, Darth Vader kind of way. (It was either that or fail English as a UFO alien vampire witch—something she doubted would be all that attractive to the Chad Steels of the world.)

Of course the writing might have been easier if she didn't have two time-traveling goofballs floating cross-legged at opposite ends of her desk.

"This is really torked, Your Babe-ness."

"Herby, please," she said, running her hands through her hair. "I'm trying to concentrate."

"Perhaps you should concentrate on telling Miss Grumpaton the truth, instead of attempting to cover it up," Tuna suggested.

"And get an F on the book report?" TJ snapped. "No way."

Tuna frowned. A moment of silence passed before he finally cleared his throat. "Hmm . . ."

TJ tried to ignore him.

He tried a little louder. *"Hmm . . ."*

Again she ignored him.

"HMM . . ."

"All right!" She tossed her pencil on the desk. "What is it, Tuna?"

"Oh, was I disturbing you?" he asked innocently.

She arched an eyebrow.

"It certainly wasn't my intention."

She arched the other eyebrow. (When it comes to eyebrows, TJ is ambidextrous.)

Finally Tuna spoke. "It seems rather odd—how cheating to eliminate extra work has only brought you more work. When, in reality, there would have been less work if you had hadn't cheated."

"You mean if *we* hadn't cheated," she corrected. "Remember, you're the ones who got me into this mess."

"That's totally right, Your Dude-ness," Herby agreed. "And we want to be the ones to get you out."

"Not this time," she said returning to her work. Then, hesitating, she looked back to him. "Unless you want to help me write the essay."

"Really?" Herby chirped excitedly. "That would be so outloopish! We could transport some super genius here to your room, and—"

"Ahem," Tuna said, trying to get his attention.

"—he could write something stupenderous, and, and—"

"*AHEM,*" Tuna repeated.

Herby glanced over to see Tuna shaking his head.

Herby suddenly caught on and sighed, "And that would be cheating again, wouldn't it?"

Tuna nodded. "And cheating is bad because . . . ?" He waited for Herby to answer.

Herby scrunched his face into a frown.

Tuna repeated the question a little slower. "And cheating is bad because . . . ?"

Herby's face brightened. "Because it's cheating!"

Tuna dropped his head into his hands and slowly shook it.

Suddenly there was a

knock, **KNOCK,** knock

at the door, followed by Dorie's squeaky little voice. "TJ?"

"What is it, Squid?" TJ called.

"When are we going to the beach?"

"The beach?"

"You said we were going swimming today, remember?"

TJ's heart sank. "I'm sorry, Dorie. But I've got way too much homework to do."

"But . . . you promised."

The disappointment in her sister's voice made TJ feel even worse. "Yeah, I know I promised. Maybe later. Okay?"

"Okay." It was obvious Dorie was trying to sound hopeful. But it was also obvious she'd failed miserably. And then, just before she walked away, there was a faint scraping sound.

TJ turned and saw a squished piece of pizza sliding under her door. "What's that?" she called.

"Pizza from last night," Dorie said. "I snucked it home 'cause I knew you'd want some."

If TJ was feeling bad before, she was feeling downright miserable now.

"I'll see you later," Dorie said.

"Yeah," TJ sighed. "Later."

With that, Dorie's little footsteps turned and faded as they headed down the hall.

TJ closed her eyes. But she had work to do. So she reopened them, ignored the heaviness in her chest, and returned to writing.

CHAPTER TEN

Ahoy, Ye Surfers!

TIME TRAVEL LOG:
Malibu, California, October 23

Begin Transmission:
Sometimes even major babes must learn the hard
way.

End Transmission

The surf meet was quite a production. Chad guessed
there were over a thousand people scattered up
and down the beach—along with food vendors,
T-shirt sellers, volleyball players, and a local TV crew,
which of course meant Hesper Breakahart and her

posse were there, pretending to cheer Chad on (while making sure they were always in front of the cameras).

The surfboard had performed flawlessly—no problems, no surprises, no nuclear holocausts. Chad had made it through all the qualifying rounds and now he was about to begin the finals.

"It's gonna be incredible!" Doug said, gulping down a soda. "You're going to *(sniff-sniff)* shut them all down and become regional champ." *(BURP!—* Doug never passed up the opportunity to try out new bodily sound effects.)

Chad grinned. "You think so?"

"We know so," Naomi said. "And after that *(click, clack)* we're off to the national *(crunch)* championships!"

Chad nodded as he looked out over the water. He still felt bad about cheating, but not nearly as bad since he was winning. Suddenly something caught his attention. "Hey, isn't that the new kid's sister?"

"Who?" Doug *sniff*-ed.

"Where?" Naomi *click*-ed.

"Out there, wading in the surf. She's pretty young. Somebody should be with her."

Doug spotted her and shrugged. "She'll be fine. I'm sure TJ's around to—"

He was interrupted by the PA announcement:

"ALL FINALISTS INTO THE WATER, PLEASE. THIS IS FOR THE FINAL ROUND. I REPEAT, THE FINAL ROUND."

"Let's go," Doug said.

Chad continued looking after the little sister. "Yeah, but—"

"Don't worry," Naomi said. "She'll be fine. You need to focus all your concentration on winning this meet."

Reluctantly, Chad nodded. He picked up his board and, with Doug's help, limped toward the water.

* * * * *

That same morning, TJ decided not to go to church with her family. She had two reasons:

1. She was lost in an avalanche of crumpled papers.
2. She figured God might work something into the pastor's sermon to remind her she

shouldn't be doing what she was doing.
(He can be tricky that way.)

But as she was about to discover, God has plenty
of other ways to make a point.

It all started with Dad dropping Dorie off after
church and going out to lunch with Violet. Part of
his *quality family time* routine was having a date with
each of his daughters once a week. That was cool.

What was not cool was TJ's turning on the local
TV station and seeing Chad in the competition.
She'd hoped he would be more honest than that.
Then again, how could she blame him? Wasn't she
being just as dishonest?

(See what I mean about God being tricky? And
if you think that's something, hang on. He was just
warming up.)

Truth be told, it was kinda fun to see Chad on TV.

More truth be told, it was *not* kinda fun seeing
Hesper Breakahart and all her wannabes posing for
the cameras in their super-expensive, super-sheer,
super-are-those-really-swimsuits-or-are-they-wearing-
dental-floss? swimwear. It was even less than not
kinda fun when TJ caught a glimpse of a child splash-
ing and playing at the water's edge. A child who
looked exactly like . . .

"Dorie!" TJ cried. Obviously, her sister had sneaked off and gone to the beach on her own. "Tuna! Herby!"

Immediately the boys

ChUgga-chugga-Chugga

BLING!-ed

into her room from their place in the attic.

"We gotta save Dorie!" TJ shouted. "She's at the beach by herself and she can't swim!"

"Say no more," Herby said. He reached for the trusty Swiss Army Knife, pulled out a blade, and they

ChUgga-chugga-Chugga

BLING!-ed

right to the

glug-glug-glug

. . . well, it was supposed to be the beach. But by the looks of things, they were at the bottom of the

Pacific Ocean! (Either that or the whales drifting by had just learned to fly.)

"HERB-BLUB-BLUB-BLUB-Y!" TJ shouted.

Herb-blub-y reached back to his knife and

Chugga-chugga-*chugga*

BLING!-ed

The good news was they landed on the beach.

The bad news was Long John Silver and his noisy

"Pieces of eight! Pieces of eight!"

parrot had appeared, too.

The badder news (don't try that word on Miss Grumpaton) was he was pointing his pistol at a volleyball player who was about to serve.

"Hand over that cannonball, matey, before I blow ye to kingdom come."

"Cannonball?" the player laughed nervously. "It's a volleyball!"

The pirate cocked his pistol and growled, "I don't care what ye naked natives call it. I need more ammo fer me ship."

"But—"

Suddenly TJ spotted Dorie. "There she is!" She pointed at the little girl, who was already in the surf, being pulled out into the ocean. TJ took off for her, yelling, "Dorie! Dorie!"

Meanwhile, Tuna and Herby both knew they had to get rid of Long John Silver for good. Unfortunately they had separate plans. Unfortunatelier (another word to hide from Miss Grumpaton), they put their plans into action at exactly the same time.

Tuna pulled out the Swiss Army Time Freezer Blade (sold at 23rd-century time-travel stores everywhere) and fired it

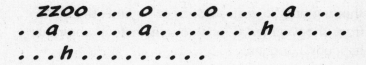

at the pirate, the same instant Herby pulled out his 3D Calculator, entered the calculations, and tried to

beekle-*deekle*

subtract Long John Silver to 0.

But as usual, the equipment

fizzle . . . fizzle . . . fizzle-ed

So instead of being subtracted to 0, Long John Silver was multiplied to 1,304.

"Argh!" 1,304 Long John Silvers *argh*-ed.

"Pieces of eight! Pieces of eight!" 1,304 parrots screamed.

And remember the Time Freezer? Well, not being the best aim, Tuna missed Long John Silver and the beam bounced off his pistol (which had turned to 1,304 pistols), reflecting the beam 1,304 different directions.

No problem, except the Time Freezer was also shorting out. So, instead of freezing time, the beam froze the weather! (Don't you just hate it when that happens?) Suddenly . . .

—the temperature dropped to -10 degrees

—the gentle ocean breeze turned into a snowy blizzard

—Hesper and all her friends turned blue and were covered in gross goose bumps . . . which meant running from the TV crew screaming, "Don't let the cameras see us! Don't let the cameras see us!"

Meanwhile, Chad had just caught the perfect
wave and began working it for the perfect score . . .
until he spotted the new kid swimming out from
the beach. He tried ignoring her—after all, he was in
the middle of winning the finals. But then he heard
her shouting.

"Dorie . . . Dorie!"

He looked to where she was swimming and spotted her little sister doing a terrible imitation of not
drowning. Again, he tried to focus on the competition. He'd worked too long and hard to be distracted.

"TJ!" the little girl screamed.

He threw another look in her direction.

Doug's voice crackled through his earpiece. *"What
are you doing? Focus, Chad! Focus!"*

"TJ, help me!"

"If you quit now, you'll lose!"

"HELP ME!" The little sister began coughing and
choking. *"HELP ME!"*

That was it. Chad made his decision. He pulled
out of the wave, dropped to his knees, and began
paddling toward the two of them.

Back on the beach, Herby, who still had this
strange belief that he could actually help, tried the
calculator again and suddenly there were

beekle-deekle

*fizzle . . . fizzle . . .
fizzle . . .*

1,304 volleyballs blowing in the blizzard and slamming everyone in the head.

Well, not everyone; mostly blue, goose-bumpy girls in dental floss swimsuits who kept running around in the wind screaming, "Don't let the cameras see us! Don't—

THUMP!

let the—"

THUMP! THUMP! THUMP!

Tuna yelled over the noise, "The Morph Blade! The calculator's not working! I'll try the Morph Blade!"

"Stupenderous idea!" Herby shouted.

Unfortunately, the knife was doing its usual shorting-out routine, which would explain why all the surfboards became

krinkle . . . krackle

POOF!

mini pirate ships.

(If it matters, we're at about 9.9 on the Weirdness Scale.)

Meanwhile, back in the ocean, TJ was exhausted. Her arms and legs were giving out. Dorie had managed to grab one of the stray volleyballs floating past, and it helped a little. It would have helped a lot if it didn't have a giant hole pecked into it by one of the 1,304 parrots. She was only 50 feet ahead of TJ, but it could have just as easily been 50 miles.

How could I have been so stupid? TJ thought. *I promised to take Dorie swimming over and over again, but I never had time because of—*

"Help me! TJ, HELP ME!" Dorie choked.

And now she's going to drown. Now we're both going to drown . . . all because of my stupid, stupid cheating!

"TJ!"

"Hang on!" she coughed. "HANG ON!"

But it did no good. TJ had nothing left. Her arms and legs finally quit working. It was over. It was all over, and it was all her fault. With her heart breaking, she started to sink. She slipped under the water, hating herself, figuring this was what she deserved . . . when a hand reached down to her. Desperately, she grabbed it. She hung on for all she was worth as it pulled her up out of the water. A moment later she was lying on the deck of a . . . *mini pirate ship?!*

Confused, she looked up, expecting to see some crazed pirate. Instead, she saw . . .

"Chad?" She coughed. "What are you doing on this thing?"

"I'm not sure!" he shouted. Before he could say any more, they were suddenly

THump! thump! THump!-ed

with a dozen volleyballs.

Surprised, TJ rose to see they were surrounded by other mini pirate ships—lots of them, all manned by surfers. And instead of firing cannons at each other, they were firing . . . you guessed it . . . volleyballs.

(For those of you keeping score, that Weirdness Scale is now at 11.7 . . . and rising.)

It was like some giant game of dodgeball. The air was full of them, as every ship shot

whish, whish, Whish

volleyballs at every other ship.

"TJ!"

She turned to see little Dorie still thrashing in the water, trying to stay afloat. The good news was she was only a few yards ahead of them. The bad news was there was a pirate ship directly between them.

"Grab those volleyballs!" Chad shouted.

"What?"

He motioned to the balls floating in the water. "Grab them and fire at that ship. I gotta steer around it and save your sister!"

(Now we're up to 13.9.)

Without hesitation, TJ scooped up a volleyball and threw it at the ship.

THump!

Of course the ship returned fire.

THump! THump!

And of course, TJ fired back.

THUMP! *THUMP!* thump!

"Attagirl!" Chad shouted as she kept throwing the balls. "Keep it up!"

At last they broke past the ship and pulled alongside Dorie.

Chad leaned out to her and shouted, "Grab my hand!"

"*Glug, glug, glug!*" Dorie *glug*-ed.

Chad stretched for all he was worth until, finally . . . "Gotcha!" He pulled her from the water.

Of course Dorie did the usual coughing and choking routine (which tends to happen when your lungs are full of water). And of course TJ threw her arms around her and did the usual sobbing and crying routine (which tends to happen when you almost lose someone you love).

"Oh, Dorie, I'm so sorry," TJ cried.

"*Cough, cough, choke, choke,*" Dorie replied.

And then, just when things were getting way too sappy, they heard

Raaaapha . . .
Reeeepha . . . Riiiipha . . .
BOING-oing-oing-OING-oing!

which, as you might recall, was the sound of one Reverse Beam Blade being activated. And if you couldn't tell by the cheap sound effects, you could tell by the

!рминт !РМинт !рминт

"!EM PLEH, JT"

!fOOP

elkcark . . . elknirk

"!su ees saremac eht tel t'noD !su ees saremac eht tel t'noD"

. . . elzzif . . . *elzzif* . . . elzzif

elkeed-elkeeb

"*!thgie fo seceiP !thgie fo seceiP*"

. . . . h . . . . h . . .
. . . . . . a . . . . . a . . . . . a . . .
. . o . . . . . o . . . oozZ

"!Y-BULB-BULB-BULB-BREH"

!GNILB

agguhc-agguhc-agguhc

until, finally, TJ had traveled so far back in time that she was back in her own bed waking up.

Amazing! Incredible! (And by now, completely off the Weirdness Scale.) Everything was just the same as when she first woke up that morning. *Nothing* was different.

But it soon would be.

tap, tap, tap

"TJ?" little Dorie's voice squeaked from the other side of the door. "You awake?"

TJ coughed and cleared her throat. "What do you want, Squid?"

"You coming to church with us?"

A smile slowly spread across TJ's face. The boys had sent her back from her own future. She'd get a second chance. And this time she'd do it right.

"TJ?"

"Yeah," she said, throwing off her covers. "Just give me a sec to get dressed."

"Cool. And maybe, maybe . . ." Dorie's little voice began getting excited. "Maybe after that, we could go to the beach?"

"You bet." TJ chuckled as she headed across the room toward her closet. "I wouldn't miss it for the world."

CHAPTER ELEVEN

Mopping Up

TIME TRAVEL LOG:
Malibu, California, October 23—TAKE TWO

Begin Transmission:
Thanks to our incredible genius and great skills,
subject has finally done things our way. Which, for
some unexplained reason, actually worked.

End Transmission

"Don't go out too far," TJ shouted to her little sister.

"Please . . . ," Dorie begged, "just a little farther,
please . . ."

Of course she used the exact whine described

in the *Little Sisters Can be Such a Pain Handbook*. The whine listed right next to such requirements as:

—Little sisters must use the bathroom at the most inconvenient times. (Usually in the middle of a movie you've finally agreed to take them to.)
—Little sisters must sneak into your closet and steal your clothes. (Then put them on and act like they were theirs in the first place.)
—Little sisters must spy on your friends whenever they come over. (Especially if the friend happens to be a boy.)

"I won't drown," Dorie begged. "Pleeeeease? I promise."

"You heard me."

"Oh, all right."

Granted, only letting Dorie wade up to her ankles might be overly cautious and extreme. But after all that had happened today (or hadn't happened today), TJ wasn't taking any chances. In fact, after her little field trip through Weirdville, she decided it was time to make some other extreme decisions as well.

—Today, the beach with Dorie
—Tomorrow, the truth with Miss Grumpaton

(and, no doubt, after-school detention for the rest
of her life)

"It won't be too zworked," Herby said, floating
beside her above the sand.

"He's right," Tuna agreed, floating at her other
side. "You really are doing the correct thing."

"I suppose," TJ sighed. "I just wish I could have
learned without all the drama."

"It does keep things interesting," Tuna said.

"And it'll look fantabulous in our history report,"
Herby said. Then, with a sigh, he added, "If we ever
do get home."

TJ gave a small shudder at the thought. It was
true; they'd been here for almost two weeks now,
and their time-travel pod was still no closer to being
repaired. She didn't want to be rude, but the sooner
they left, the sooner her life would return to normal.

"Hey!"

They turned to see Chad Steel hobbling down the
beach toward them.

"Oh no," TJ whispered, "what do I do?"

"Converse with him," Tuna whispered.

"Unless you want to send him to that school of
whales we saw earlier today," Herby said, reaching
for his Swiss Army Knife.

"No!" TJ gasped. "Put that away!"

"I'm sorry—" Chad frowned—"what'd you say?"

TJ swallowed and looked another direction.

He tried again. "I thought that was you down here."

She nodded. There was nothing but silence.

Spotting Dorie, he asked, "Is that your little sister?"

She nodded. Nothing but more silence.

They watched a moment as Dorie kicked and splashed, having the time of her life in three inches of water.

"Cute kid," he said.

More nodding. Even more silence.

It was deafening. At least to TJ. But as far as she could tell, Chad was perfectly comfortable with the silence. And why wouldn't he be? He wasn't the one worried about how stupid he looked in a one-piece bathing suit, or why his hair always frizzed in the ocean air, or why he always came down with a bad case of muteness whenever he was around.

"Why aren't you watching the surfing match?" he asked.

Instead of nodding, TJ tried something brand-new, a revolutionary approach. She shrugged.

"There are some pretty good surfers competing," he said a little sadly.

Suddenly it dawned on her. He wasn't there. And before she could catch herself, she croaked, "What about you?"

He shook his head. "Not this time."

"Why not?" she asked, still sounding more frog than human.

It was Chad's turn to shrug. "Actually, you and your little sister—you guys were part of the reason."

TJ didn't understand.

He explained. "I had the weirdest dream. I was competing in the match—you know, cheating like we talked about a couple nights back?"

TJ returned to auto-nod.

"And I was just about to win, when I looked over my shoulder and saw your sister drowning."

TJ swallowed, but her mouth was as dry as leather. Of course it hadn't been a dream, but she wasn't about to tell him that.

"And for a moment, I didn't care. I know that sounds awful, but at that moment all I wanted to do was win."

Again TJ tried to swallow, but her mouth was now as dry as leather stuck in a clothes dryer on high

for three days in the middle of the Sahara Desert
(on a very warm day).

"And that's when it hit me. It's like the more I was
cheating, the less I cared about doing the right thing,
until . . . well, until I cared more about winning than
I cared about people."

TJ said nothing. It's hard talking when your heart
has leaped into your throat.

Chad looked down at the sand. "Pretty creepy,
huh."

Once again she felt her eyes start to burn with
tears. And once again she gave them a swipe.

"You okay?" he asked.

She nodded.

"Must be allergies or something," he said.

More nodding and more swiping.

"Come on, Your Babe-ness," Herby whispered
beside her. "Say something."

But there was no way TJ could talk. They'd both
gone through the exact same thing. Together, but
separately. Unbelievable. She wiped her eyes again.
And then, just when she thought of blurting out what
really happened, telling him about Tuna and Herby,
pouring out her heart (and explaining how utterly
and completely perfect they were for each other),
she heard a very familiar and very unwelcome voice:

"Hey, Chad, there you are!"

She looked up to see Elizabeth standing with her hands on her very slim and very perfect hips.

"Hesper's waiting for you up the beach."

Chad nodded. He glanced up the beach, then looked back to TJ. "Listen, maybe we can get something to eat sometime. You know, just to talk."

If TJ's heart was in her throat before, it had now leaped out of her mouth.

"Talk?" she repeated in her best Kermit the Frog voice.

"Yeah. I mean, that's what friends do, right? . . . Talk?"

TJ nodded, also hoping "friends" would call the paramedics, bring in the life-support systems, and jump-start her heart, which had not only leaped out of her mouth but was now flopping around all over the sand.

"Chad," Elizabeth said, "are you coming or what?"

He ignored her and continued speaking to TJ. "I can understand if you don't want to—I mean, with me being such a creep and all, wanting to cheat and everything like that."

"But you didn't cheat," TJ croaked.

Chad looked at her, thought a moment, then slowly started to nod. "Yeah, I guess you're right.

I didn't, did I?" He thought another moment, then chuckled.

Somehow she was able to hold his gaze.

"But only 'cause of that dream I had about you and your sister."

That was it. That was all she could stand. She felt her ears starting to burn and looked away.

He gave another chuckle. "See what a positive influence you are on me?"

Forget the burning ears; now her entire face was on fire.

"Even when I sleep."

And forget about those paramedics—it was time to call out the fire engines.

"Chad," Elizabeth demanded, "you know how Hesper hates waiting."

Chad sighed heavily. "Well, give it some thought. Getting something to eat, I mean." Then without a word, he finally turned and started hobbling back up the beach toward Hesper and her beauty queens.

TJ looked on, staring with amazement. The moment had been unbelievable . . . perfect. Well, almost perfect. There was still the little problem of Elizabeth. Once Chad was out of earshot, the girl immediately moved in and gave TJ a piece of her mind.

"You're not fooling anyone, you know."

"I'm sorry?"

"With your spells or alien mumbo jumbo or whatever."

"I don't understand."

"Making everyone have the same dream last night. I mean, honestly, did you think I wouldn't find out?"

TJ only stared.

"But just so you know, I'm still going to expose you. I'm gonna make sure *everyone* knows exactly who or *what* you are."

"Not from the bottom of the sea you won't," Herby said, reaching for his knife.

"What did you say?" Elizabeth asked in surprise.

"No, Herby!" TJ cried. "Don't!"

But she was too late. Suddenly

Chugga-chugga-chugga

BLING!

Elizabeth was gone.

"What have you done?!" TJ shouted. "Where is she?"

Tuna guessed, "Doing a little whale watching, is she?"

"That's right, dude," Herby chuckled. "Up real close and personal."

"You can't do that!" TJ cried. "She'll drown."

Herby frowned. "Oh yeah." Then, reaching for the knife, he said, "Guess we'll have to morph her some

krinkle . . . **krackle**

POOF!

gills and fish fins."

"Herby!"

He pouted. "Well . . . all right. I guess we don't wanna scare the whales." With that he

chugga-chugga-chugga

BLING!-ed

Elizabeth back out of the water and onto the beach to join Hesper and all her friends . . . who suddenly broke out into a bad case of

"Eeek!"s

"AWKkk!"s

and a whole lot of

"Shrieeeek"s

"Now what did you do?" TJ demanded.

Herby shrugged. "I might have forgotten to remove her gills and fins."

"Herby!"

"Oh, all right," he sighed. Once again he reached for his Swiss Army Knife.

And as Herby prepared to turn everything back to normal, TJ somehow feared—no, she somehow *knew*—that normal would not be something she would be experiencing for a very long time. Until then, TJ Finkelstein would be your average, run-of-the-mill seventh grader plagued by two very sweet but very clueless time stumblers from the 23rd century.

Turn the page for a sneak peek at

OOPS!

the next wacky adventure in the TJ and
the Time Stumblers series by Bill Myers.

CHAPTER ONE

Beginnings . . .

TIME TRAVEL LOG:
Malibu, California, November 2

Begin Transmission:
All-school bully from the future stopped by. Despite his disguise, Tuna and I are positive it's Bruce Bruiseabone, winner of the Worst Breath in the World Contest. We fear he could really zwork things up for our subject (who, by the way, is still smoot to the max).

End Transmission

Thelma Jean Finkelstein, better known as TJ to her friends (all four of them—unless you leave out her goldfish and pet hamster, which brings it down to two friends), ran through the empty cafeteria, screaming her lungs out.

"AHHHHHHH!"

And when she wasn't

"AHHHHHHH!"-ing

she was yelling,

"Why is he chasing us?"

"Why is he chasing us?!"

Now, you might call her behavior a little weird (which may be why she has only two friends). But weirder than that weirdness is that the **HE** in her little screamfest just happened to be an African elephant the size of a Chevy pickup who, unlike a Chevy pickup, had some very bad breath.

Weirder than *that* weirdness was that the African elephant (complete with large tusks and

a crummy mood) was shouting in a very bad British
accent,

**"Excuse me, miss. If you don't mind, I
should like to speak with you a moment!"**

Weirder than *that* weird weirdness was the **US** TJ
happened to be screaming about. And who, exactly,
was the **US**?

Actually, they were nobody. (Unless you counted
the two invisible teenagers from the 23rd century
who were running beside her.)

First, there was Thomas Uriah Norman Alphonso
the Third. Or for those who don't enjoy spraining
their tongues, Tuna. On TJ's other side ran Herby,
a tall surfer dude with long blond bangs and the
exact same number of brain cells as TJ had friends
(*after* you subtract the goldfish and hamster).

The boys had traveled back in time to do a
history report on TJ because, believe it or not,
someday when she was through screaming her
lungs out and being chased by African elephants
through school cafeterias, TJ would become a
great world leader.

But until then, she had other things on her mind like:

"AHHHHHHH!"

Get us out of here!

Get us out of here!"

"No worries, Your Dude-ness," Herby shouted. "I'll transport us home!" With that he pulled out his trusty Swiss Army Knife (sold at 23rd-century time-travel stores everywhere), opened its Transporter Beam Blade and

chugga-chugga-chugga

BLING!

The good news was Herby transported them out of the cafeteria.

The bad news was he missed TJ's house (unless she had moved to the top of Mount Everest).

The top of Mount Everest! you say?

Yeah, that's what TJ was saying too. Only more like:

"THE TOP OF MOUNT EVEREST!"

"How odd!" Tuna yelled over the howling wind.

"That we're on Mount Everest?" Herby shouted. "Or that the elephant is still behind us?"

"Actually, I'm talking about the end of the giant glacier we're approaching."

"What end?" Herby shouted. "What glacier?"

"The end we've just reached and the glacier we are now jumping

O
F
F
!"

Wanting to be part of the conversation, TJ threw in her own comment—the always clever and very appropriate

"A
H
H
!"

OOPS!

And refusing to be left out, the elephant, who was
falling beside them, added,

"I

 d
  o

 b
  e
   l
    i
     e
      v
       e

       t
        h
         i
          s

    m
     a
      y

h
u
r
t
a
b
i
t
!"

But thanks to Herby's great thinking (and accidental good luck), he tried the Transporter Beam Blade again and

chugga-chugga-chugga

instead of hitting the ground, they

BLING!-ed

back to school and were running down the hallway toward the auditorium.

That was the good news. But as you may recall,

every time TJ gets a little good news, she gets a ton of bad. In this case, it came in the form of one African elephant (whose breath had not improved) who was still running after them. And (since we're having a two-for-one special in TJ's bad luck department) there was the added problem of Hesper Breakahart, star of her own TV series on the Dizzy Channel (and the richest, most gorgeous, most spoiled 13-year-old in the entire civilized world— and maybe Texas, too). At the moment she was inside that very auditorium holding auditions for her TV show.

* * * * *